Snowed In with the Mountain Doctor

An Angel Peak Steamy Instalove Novella

Ellie Masters

Master of Romantic Suspense

JEM Publishing

DEDICATION

This book is dedicated to my one and only—my amazing and wonderful husband.

Without your care and support, my writing would not have made it this far.

You pushed me when I needed to be pushed.

You supported me when I felt discouraged.

You believed in me when I didn't believe in myself.

If it weren't for you, this book never would have come to life.

ALSO BY ELLIE MASTERS

The LIGHTER SIDE

Ellie Masters is the lighter side of the Jet & Ellie Masters writing duo! You will find Contemporary Romance, Military Romance, Romantic Suspense, Billionaire Romance, and Rock Star Romance in Ellie's Works.

YOU CAN FIND ELLIE'S BOOKS HERE:

ELLIEMASTERS.COM/BOOKS

SUGGESTED READING ORDER

START HERE

Rockstar Romance

The Angel Fire Rock Romance Series

EACH BOOK IN THIS SERIES CAN BE READ AS A STANDALONE AND IS ABOUT A DIFFERENT COUPLE WITH AN HEA. IT IS RECOMMENDED THEY ARE READ IN ORDER.

Heart's Insanity

Ashes to New

Heart's Desire

Heart's Collide

Hearts Divided

Hearts Entwined

Forest's FALL

Hearts The Last Beat

CONTINUE HERE...

Rescuing Malia

Rescuing Ally

Delta Team (Coming Soon)

Rescuing Ember

Rescuing Aria

STANDALONES IN THE GUARDIAN HOSTAGE RESCUE SERIES YOU CAN READ ANYTIME

Military Romance

Guardian Personal Protection Specialists

Sybil's Protector

Lyra's Protector

Angel Peak Steamy Instalove Novella Series

(Small Town)

By Ellie Masters

EACH BOOK IN THIS SERIES CAN BE READ AS A STANDALONE AND IS ABOUT A DIFFERENT COUPLE WITH AN HEA.

SNOWED IN WITH THE MOUNTAIN DOCTOR

Rescued by the Mountain Guide

Stranded with the Resort Owner

Matched with the Small-Town Chef

Trapped with the Forest Ranger

Snowbound with the Vineyard Owner

Reunited with the Hometown Hero

The One I Want Series

(Small Town, Military Heroes)

By Jet & Ellie Masters

Michelle

Ivy

HOT READS

Becoming His Series

THIS SERIES MUST BE READ IN ORDER.

The Ballet

Learning to Breathe

Becoming His

Dark Captive Romance

A STANDALONE NOVEL.

She's MINE

TO MY READERS

This book is a work of fiction. It does not exist in the real world and should not be construed as reality. As in most romantic fiction, I've taken liberties. I've compressed the romance into a sliver of time. I've allowed these characters to develop strong bonds of trust over a matter of days.

This does not happen in real life where you, my amazing readers, live. Take more time in your romance and learn who you're giving a piece of your heart to. I urge you to move with caution. Always protect yourself.

Angel's Peak

Angel's Peak

CHAPTER 1

A MOUNTAIN DETOUR

I GRIP MY STEERING WHEEL TIGHTER AS SNOWFLAKES fall more heavily on my weekend escape to Angel's Peak. This was supposed to be a simple two-day retreat from my chaotic Denver hospital schedule—not this white-knuckle drive up increasingly treacherous mountain roads.

"Stupid, stupid, stupid," I mutter to myself as my wipers struggle against the thickening snow. "Why didn't you check the weather forecast, Tess?"

The answer is simple: because I hadn't thought beyond escaping. Three back-to-back surgeries, followed by the hospital board meeting where they not-so-subtly hinted that the department head position was mine if I "demonstrated appropriate commitment." Translation: *work yourself to death and maybe, just maybe, we'll reward you.*

So when my college roommate Jenna texted about her family's empty cabin in Angel's Peak, it seemed like the perfect getaway. No cell service. No emails. No ambitious residents seeking my approval. Just me, some novels I've been meaning to read for months, and blessed silence.

My car lurches sideways, sliding toward the guardrail, and my daydream shatters.

"No, no, no!" I wrestle with the wheel, heart pounding as I straighten out just in time. My surgeon's hands, normally steady under pressure, tremble against the leather.

That was too close. In the space of twenty minutes, this snowfall has turned into a proper blizzard, and visibility is rapidly approaching zero. I need to find shelter now.

I spot a small building with lights still on through the swirling white, just visible off the main road. I turn carefully, creeping forward until I make out a sign: "Angel's Peak Medical Clinic."

Perfect. If I have to be stranded, at least it's somewhere with heat and people who understand emergencies.

I park as close to the entrance as possible, grab my overnight bag from the passenger seat, and dash through knee-deep snow to the front door. By the time I reach it, I'm half-frozen and completely covered in fat, fluffy flakes.

The door is thankfully unlocked. I push inside, bringing a swirl of snowflakes with me, and find myself in a small, rustic waiting room. It's empty except for a potted plant and some outdated magazines.

"Hello?" I call out, my voice echoing slightly. "Is anyone here?"

"We're closed," comes a deep voice from somewhere beyond a half-open door. "Unless it's an emergency."

"It's not a medical emergency," I reply, stamping snow from my boots. "But I nearly drove off the mountain, and I don't think I can make it to my friend's cabin in this storm."

The door swings open, and the man who steps through it stops me dead in my tracks.

He's tall—six-foot-two at least—with broad shoulders filling out a dark blue henley that matches eyes so intensely blue they're visible from across the room. Dark hair, just long enough to run my fingers through, frames a face that belongs on a magazine cover, not hidden away in a mountain clinic. A day's worth of stubble accentuates a strong jaw, and when he smiles at me, I feel it like a physical touch.

"Roads getting bad?" He crosses muscular arms over his chest and for a moment, I forget how to breathe.

I nod, suddenly aware of how I must look—hair wild from the wind, makeup probably smeared, snow melting on his clean floor.

"Getting bad?" I finally manage. "They're deadly. I almost went over the edge back there."

Something shifts in his expression—a professional assessment replacing the initial wariness.

"You're not hurt?" he asks, giving me a thorough once-over that feels decidedly clinical despite the way my skin heats under his gaze.

"No. Just shaken up. And very, very lost." I hold out my hand. "I'm Dr. Tess Carrington. I was heading to my friend's cabin for the weekend."

His eyebrow raises slightly at my title, and when he takes my hand, the contact sends a jolt straight up my arm. His palm is warm and calloused, his grip confident without being crushing.

"Cole Blake, Emergency doc." He holds my hand a beat longer than necessary, and I resist the urge to pull away—not from discomfort, but because the contact is stirring something primitive I'd rather not acknowledge. "I'm covering the clinic while Dr. Reid is at a conference."

When he finally releases my hand, I tuck it safely into my pocket, trying to ignore the lingering warmth.

"Well, Dr. Blake—"

"Cole," he interrupts, the corner of his mouth lifting in what might be the beginning of a smile.

"Cole," I correct myself, surprised by how easily his name rolls off my tongue. "Can you give me directions—"

"You're not going anywhere tonight," he says with absolute certainty. "They'll have closed the mountain roads by now. A checkpoint about a mile back shuts down when conditions get dangerous."

He moves past me to the window, his arm brushing mine and leaving a trail of goosebumps I hope he doesn't notice. Pulling back the blinds, he stares out at the worsening storm.

"But I—"

"I'm afraid you're stuck with me for the night. Tell your friend you're safe but staying at the clinic." He glances at me. "You *are* safe. I'm not an axe murderer, just the doc unlucky enough to be on call during a blizzard."

I pull out my phone, already knowing what I'll find. "No service."

"Landline's over there." He points to a desk in the corner. "Dial 9 to get out."

"Guess, I'm stuck." I hang up with a sinking feeling.

Cole, who's been watching me with an unreadable expression, nods. "Looks like it."

"Is there anywhere in town I could stay? A hotel or...?"

"Everything's at the top of the mountain near the lodge. Down here it's just the clinic, a couple of shops, and local homes." He hesitates, then adds, "There's a break room with a decent couch in the back. It's where I crash when I'm on call. And there's a shower in the staff bathroom."

I bite my lip, considering my options—which are essentially nonexistent.

"I'd offer you my place," he continues, "but I live about fifteen minutes out, and my truck might not make it in this." He gestures at the worsening storm.

"The couch sounds perfect," I say quickly, relieved. "Thank you. I appreciate it."

"Don't thank me yet. It's not exactly five-star accommodation." He studies me for a moment, then asks, "What kind of doctor?"

"Trauma surgeon."

His eyes widen fractionally—either impressed or surprised, I can't tell.

"Denver General," I add, unsure why I need to establish my credentials.

"Big hospital," he comments, walking back toward the door he came through earlier. "Follow me. I'll show you where everything is."

I grab my bag and follow him down a short hallway, trying not to notice how his jeans fit perfectly over muscular thighs or how he moves with the easy confidence of a man completely at home in his own skin.

The urgent care clinic is small but surprisingly well-equipped. He points out the exam rooms, supply closet, and a tiny lab area.

"Not what you're used to, I'm sure," he says, and I detect a hint of defensiveness in his tone. "But we're trying to expand our emergency services. We get a lot from the resort. Broken bones, concussions, stuff from people pushing their limits."

"This is impressive for a town this size."

Something like approval flickers across his face. "Break room's through here."

The room is small but comfortable, with a surprisingly plush-looking couch along one wall, a mini-fridge, a microwave, and a small table with two chairs.

"Bathroom's through that door," he says, pointing. "There are clean towels in the cabinet and probably some travel-sized toiletries left by various drug reps."

"This is perfect," I tell him, meaning it. "Really."

He nods, then hesitates. "You hungry? I was about to heat some soup when you arrived."

My stomach chooses that moment to growl audibly, and I laugh, embarrassed. "I guess that's a yes."

His smile transforms his face, softening the hard edges and lighting up his eyes in a way that makes my breath catch. "Chicken noodle or tomato?"

"Surprise me," I say, dropping my bag beside the couch.

While he heads to the kitchen area, I take the opportunity to send a quick text to my friend Jenna—it won't go through until I have service again, but at least it's ready. Then, I unpack a few essentials and head to the bathroom to wash up.

The face that looks back at me from the mirror is a disaster. My normally sleek dark hair is a wild tangle, my mascara is smudged under my eyes, and my cheeks are flushed from the cold. I splash water on my face, tame my hair as best I can, and apply some tinted lip balm in a futile attempt to look less like I just survived an avalanche.

When I emerge, Cole is setting two steaming mugs on the table along with some crackers.

"Chicken noodle," he says, pushing one toward me. "And hot chocolate. Storm essentials."

"Thank you." I settle into the chair across from him. The soup is homemade, as is the hot chocolate. It's amazing and has a little kick to it I can't place. "This is really kind of you."

He shrugs one broad shoulder. "Can't exactly throw you back into the blizzard."

We eat in surprisingly comfortable silence for a few minutes before he asks, "So, what brings a Denver trauma surgeon to our little mountain town in the middle of a snowstorm?"

"Escape," I admit, cupping my hands around the warm mug. "Just needed a few days away from the hospital politics and endless hours."

He nods, understanding in his eyes. "Bad week?"

"Bad month. I'm up for department head, and it's

bringing out everyone's competitive side. Including mine," I add ruefully.

"Sounds intense."

"It is. And I want it—I've worked toward it for years—but sometimes I wonder if it's worth the constant pressure." I'm surprised by my candor. Something about his steady gaze makes it easy to talk.

"And what about you?" I ask, shifting the focus. "How does an emergency doc end up running a mountain clinic solo?" It hasn't escaped my attention he's alone. No nursing support. No front desk technician.

A shadow crosses his face. "Dr. Reid—he's the regular physician here—his wife had a stroke. Conference is just the cover story we're using to keep people from panicking. Small towns," he adds with a small smile. "Everyone worries when the only doctor leaves. As for my nurse, she's snowed in up the mountain."

"That's awful. Is she going to be okay?"

"Too soon to tell, but she's a trouper. As for Dr. Reid, he's not coming back anytime soon, so the clinic board is scrambling to find coverage."

I understand the situation all too well. Rural medicine is always hanging by a thread, and the loss of even one provider can be catastrophic for a community.

"How long have you been here?" I ask, genuinely curious.

"Three years. Came from Chicago originally."

"That's quite a change."

His eyes meet mine over the rim of his mug. "Needed my own escape, I guess."

There's a story there, but it doesn't feel like the right time to press. Instead, I take another sip of the surprisingly rich hot chocolate.

"This is delicious," I say.

"My grandmother's recipe. Real chocolate, milk, vanilla, and a pinch of cayenne."

"Cayenne?" That explains the *kick*.

"Secret ingredient." He grins, and it transforms his face again, making him look younger and more approachable.

Our hands brush as I reach for a cracker at the same time he does, and that same electric jolt shoots up my arm. This time, he feels it, too, because his eyes darken, pupils dilating in a way that has nothing to do with the dim lighting.

For a moment, we're frozen in place, the air between us suddenly charged with something that has no business existing between two strangers. I've never experienced such an immediate, visceral reaction to someone—it's like my body recognizes his on some primal level, completely bypassing my rational mind.

He breaks the contact first, clearing his throat and standing up to take his empty mug to the sink.

"I should check the emergency line and make sure we haven't missed any calls." His voice is slightly rougher than before.

"Of course." I'm grateful for the moment to collect myself. What is wrong with me? I don't react like this to men I've just met. Especially not men who work in healthcare. I have a strict "no dating colleagues" rule for good reason.

But he's not your colleague, a treacherous voice in my head points out. *Not really.*

Cole returns a few minutes later, looking more composed. "All quiet. Guess everyone's staying put in this weather."

"Smart of them." I gather our empty soup mugs. "Unlike some people."

"City drivers," he teases, some of the earlier tension fading. "Always think they can beat the mountain."

"Hey, I grew up in Colorado," I protest, following him to the small sink. "Just not in the mountains."

"Denver girl, then?"

"Born and raised. You?"

"Chicago suburbs until college. Medical school at Northwestern. Six years in the military, and worked at Rush for five years before coming here."

"That's a prestigious program," I say, genuinely impressed. "And Rush is a great hospital." Did he say military? There's another story for me, if I'm brave enough to ask.

He raises an eyebrow. "Surprised a guy would leave that for this?"

"That's not what I meant—"

"It's fine," he cuts me off, but his voice is gentle. "Most people are. But I got tired of being a small cog in a big machine. Here, I make a difference every day."

I understand that feeling all too well. It's part of why I went into trauma—immediate impact, clear results. But lately, even that hasn't been enough to counter the bureaucracy and politics.

"Anyway," he continues, checking his watch, "it's getting late. I should let you get some rest." He moves to a closet and pulls out bedding—sheets, a pillow, and a handmade quilt. "These should keep you warm. The heating's good, but it gets cold at night."

"Thank you. Again." I take the stack from him, our fingers brushing once more. This time, I don't pull away quite so quickly, and neither does he.

"If you need anything, I'll be in the on-call room next door," he says, his voice lower than before. "Just knock."

I nod, suddenly very aware of how close we're standing, of the faint scent of pine and something distinctly male that seems to surround him.

"Goodnight, Dr. Carrington," he says, stepping back.

"Tess," I correct him. "Only my patients call me Dr. Carrington."

His slow smile makes my stomach flip. "Goodnight, Tess."

"Goodnight, and thank you."

He closes the door behind him. When I turn to make up the couch, I try to shake off the lingering awareness that seems to hum beneath my skin.

It's just the adrenaline from the drive. The relief of finding shelter. The unusual situation.

But as I change into the t-shirt and shorts I sleep in and slide under the quilt, I'm lying to myself. What I felt when our eyes met and when our hands touched wasn't circumstantial. It was chemistry, pure, powerful, and potent, the kind I've read about but never truly experienced.

And what terrifies me, what keeps me staring at the ceiling long after I should be asleep, is the certainty that if I knock on his door right now, he would open it.

And neither of us would get any sleep at all.

Angel's Peak

CHAPTER 2

MEDICAL MINDS

I WAKE TO THE SMELL OF COFFEE AND THE SOUND OF voices. For a moment, I'm disoriented; the unfamiliar couch and handmade quilt are nothing like my sleek bedroom in Denver. Then yesterday's events come rushing back—the blizzard, the clinic, and Cole Blake with those impossibly blue eyes.

Sunlight streams through the small window, bouncing off what must be feet of fresh snow outside. I check my phone: It's 8:17 AM, and there's still no service. So much for my early-morning call with the hospital board.

I quickly freshen up in the bathroom, grateful for my emergency makeup bag. I'm not usually vain, but something about Cole makes me want to look my best. I tame my hair into a presentable ponytail and apply minimal makeup before venturing out toward the voices.

The clinic waiting room is occupied now—a woman holding a young boy who can't be more than four or five. The child is sniffling, tears tracking down his chubby cheeks.

"Just a few more minutes, Liam," the woman says. "Cole will make it all better."

Cole emerges from one of the exam rooms, and my breath catches. He's even more attractive in full professional mode than yesterday—now wearing dark blue scrubs that emphasize his broad shoulders and lean waist. His hair is slightly damp as if he's just showered, and the scent of his soap hits me as he walks past.

"Good morning," he says, shooting me a glance before focusing on the child. "Hey buddy, what happened to you?"

"I—I fell," the boy hiccups. "On the ice."

"Were you being a superhero again?" Cole asks gently, and the boy nods, a tiny grin breaking through his tears.

"I was The Flash."

"Well, even The Flash slips sometimes." Cole leads them toward an exam room. "Let's take a look at that arm."

As they pass, the woman—presumably Liam's mother— gives me a curious once-over, clearly wondering who I am and why I'm emerging from the staff area.

"Dr. Carrington," Cole explains, noticing the exchange. "She got caught in the storm last night and had to stay over." To me, he adds, "This is Hannah Lewis and her son Liam. The clinic's first customers of the day."

"Nice to meet you," Hannah says, her expression immediately warming at my title. "Are you joining the practice here?"

"No, I'm just—"

"She's visiting from Denver," Cole interrupts smoothly. "Big-shot trauma surgeon slumming it with us country folk."

I shoot him a look, but there's humor in his eyes that softens the remark.

"Coffee's fresh," he adds, nodding toward the break room. "Help yourself. I'll be a few minutes with our young daredevil here."

I retreat to the break room, where I find coffee and a small spread of pastries that weren't there last night. A chocolate croissant with a handwritten note sits on a folded napkin: *"Figured you for a chocolate person. –C.B."*

The gesture is oddly touching. I pour a cup of coffee and bite the croissant, closing my eyes at the buttery, chocolatey goodness. It is definitely not from a chain bakery.

When Cole reappears ten minutes later, I'm on my second cup and scrolling through emails that downloaded before I lost service.

"Arm's not broken," he announces, washing his hands at the small sink. "Just a nasty sprain. Got him wrapped up and sent them home with care instructions."

"You're good with kids."

He shrugs, pouring himself coffee. "Helps that I've known Liam since he was born. That's the thing about small towns—your patients are also your neighbors." He nods at my half-eaten croissant. "Good?"

"Amazing. Where did you get these?"

"Margie's Bakery, down the street. Owner's husband had a heart attack last year. I helped stabilize him until the helicopter came, so she makes sure I never go hungry." He leans against the counter, studying me. "Sleep okay?"

"Better than I expected," I admit. "Any update on the roads?"

"Plows are working, but it'll be midday at least before they open the roads up the mountain. You're stuck with me a while longer, I'm afraid."

Something in his tone makes me look up sharply. His professional demeanor with his patient softens, and the warmth in his gaze sends a flutter through my stomach.

"I've been in worse places." I aim for casual and miss by a mile.

"So have I." His smile is slow and knowing, as if he can read every inappropriate thought I'm trying not to have.

Before I can respond, the phone rings. He pushes off the

counter to answer it, and I take the moment to collect myself. What is wrong with me? I'm behaving like a lovesick teenager, not a thirty-two-year-old professional woman.

When Cole returns, his expression shifts to concern. "That was Sam Wilson—local with diabetes. His pump's malfunctioning, and his blood sugar's dropping. He lives about ten minutes from here, but with the roads—"

"You need to make a house call," I finish for him.

He nods, already moving toward the coat rack. "I'd normally close the clinic, but since you're here..."

"You want me to cover?" I raise an eyebrow. "I'm not licensed in ER medicine."

"Just need someone to answer the phone and tell people I'll be back in an hour. Any real emergencies get directed to regional dispatch for the helicopter." He pulls on a heavy parka. "Unless you'd rather come with me? Snow's pretty deep, though."

For a moment, I consider it—the adventure of a mountain house call, more time with Cole—but professionalism wins out.

"I'll hold down the fort," I say. "Just show me what I need to know about the phones."

He walks me through the simple system, then hesitates by the door, snow boots and medical bag in hand.

"Thanks for this," he says. "Most city doctors wouldn't bother."

"I'm happy to help."

Something passes between us, a moment of mutual understanding that feels more intimate than it should.

"Back soon," he says, and then he's gone, the door closing behind him with a soft click.

I spend twenty minutes answering emails and checking the news on my tablet before the clinic door chimes again.

"Cole?" calls a woman's voice.

"He's on a house call," I reply, emerging from the break room. "He should be back within the hour."

The newcomer is elderly, at least in her eighties, bundled in a heavy coat and woolen hat. A man of similar age stands beside her, looking worried.

"It's my prescription," the woman explains. "I'm completely out, and with the roads the way they are, we can't get to the pharmacy in Riverdale."

"I'm Dr. Carrington." I step forward. "I'm covering while Cole—um, Dr. Blake—is out. What prescription do you need?"

"Blood pressure medication," she says. "I've been taking it for twenty years. Never missed a day until now."

"Let me see what I can do. Come in and get warm."

I lead them to the waiting area and take a moment to think. The clinic must have some kind of emergency dispensary, but I have no idea where it is or how it's organized.

"I'm just going to check the records." I move to the computer behind the reception desk.

The system is password-protected, of course. I try "Angels-Peak" and "MedicalClinic" with no luck. On a hunch, I type "ChicagoBears"—remembering Cole mentioned growing up near Chicago—and I'm in. Mental note: lecture him about password security later.

I find the patient records easily enough—Martha and George Washington, which can't possibly be their real names but makes me smile nonetheless. Martha's prescription is for a common beta-blocker, nothing unusual.

The dispensary turns out to be a locked cabinet in the supply room. The key, thankfully, is hanging on a hook labeled "Meds" near the computer. Inside, medications are organized alphabetically, and I quickly find what I need, checking and double-checking the dosage against her chart.

I've just finished dispensing a week's supply and reviewing

the medication with Martha when the clinic door opens again, bringing in a blast of cold air and a snow-covered Cole.

His eyes widen slightly at the scene—me behind the counter, pill bottle in hand, the elderly couple seated in the waiting area.

"Everything okay?" He shrugs off his parka.

"Just helping Mrs. Washington with her prescription," I explain. "She was out of her beta-blocker."

Martha beams at him. "Your doctor friend is very efficient, Cole. She's very pretty. You should ask her out."

I choke back a laugh as Cole's ears turn pink. "Mrs. Washington flirts with all the medical staff." He helps the couple up. "How did you get here, Martha? Did George drive in this weather?"

"Our grandson dropped us off on his way to check the generator at the church," George says. "He'll be back in an hour."

"Then you're staying for coffee," Cole declares, leading them to the break room. "Doctor's orders."

I follow, charmed by the easy way he interacts with them and the genuine concern beneath his teasing. This is what I miss most in my hospital practice—the continuity of care and really knowing patients as people.

While Cole sets up the Washingtons with coffee and pastries, I return to the dispensary to properly log the medication I dispensed. A few minutes later, he joins me there, standing close enough that I can feel the cold still emanating from his clothes.

"You figured out the system." He sounds impressed.

"It wasn't exactly rocket science."

"Still. Most specialists wouldn't bother." He lowers his voice. "How'd you get past the password?"

I smile innocently. "Lucky guess. Bears fan?"

"Die-hard. And yes, I know it's a terrible password."

"Practically malpractice," I agree solemnly.

He laughs, and the sound does something warm and dangerous to my insides. "I'll change it immediately, Dr. Carrington."

"See that you do."

We're standing too close in the small dispensary, the banter taking on a flirtatious edge neither of us is trying very hard to disguise. His attention shifts to my lips for a fraction of a second before he steps back.

"How was your house call?" I ask, following him back to the front desk.

"Typical Sam—waited until he was bottoming out before calling. Got his pump reset and gave him a lecture he'll ignore until next time." He glances at the Washingtons, happily munching pastries in the break room. "Thanks for handling things here."

"It was nothing. Really."

"Not nothing," he counters. "You didn't have to step in like that."

Something about his sincere gratitude makes me uncomfortable. I'm not used to such straightforward appreciation without an agenda attached.

"Anyway," I say, changing the subject, "any update on the roads?"

"Actually, yes. Got a text from the sheriff while I was at Sam's. They're making good progress—should have access to the lodge by early afternoon. I'm sure you can get a room there and salvage something of your weekend."

"Oh." I'm surprised by my disappointment. "That's... good."

Cole studies me, his expression unreadable. "Unless you'd rather stay another night?"

The question hangs between us, loaded with implications. Before I can respond, the phone rings again, saving me from deciding whether the invitation is a professional courtesy or something more.

The morning passes in a blur after that. The clinic suddenly gets busy—nothing serious, but a steady stream of locals taking advantage of the partially cleared roads to handle minor concerns they'd been putting off. A sore throat. A rash. A twisted ankle from an ill-advised attempt to shovel a driveway.

I work alongside Cole as if we've been partners for years. I take the more complex cases while he handles the routine ones. Our styles complement each other surprisingly well. He's more thorough than I expected, with an excellent diagnostic mind and an intuitive understanding of patients that can't be taught in medical school.

By lunchtime, we've cleared the waiting room, and I'm energized in a way I haven't felt at work in months. Cole seems to notice, shooting me curious glances as we clean up the exam rooms.

"What?" I finally ask, catching him staring.

"You're smiling," he says. "Really smiling. Not the polite doctor face."

I hadn't realized, but he's right. "I guess I am."

"Looks good on you." He tosses a used glove into the bin with perfect aim. "You don't smile much in Denver, do you?"

The observation is too perceptive, cutting straight to a truth I've been avoiding.

"Not lately, no."

He doesn't press, just nods as if I've confirmed something he already suspected. "Hungry? I've got sandwiches in the fridge. Or we could walk down to the café if you want to stretch your legs. Roads are clear enough for that, at least."

"Sandwiches sound great," I say, taking the safer option.

If he's disappointed, he doesn't show it. "Coming right up."

In the break room, he pulls out a surprisingly sophisticated lunch—not just sandwiches but a small container of soup and what appears to be homemade pasta salad.

"Did Margie provide this too?" I ask as he sets the food on the table.

"No, I did." At my raised eyebrow, he adds, "What, men can't cook?"

"I didn't say that."

"You didn't have to. Your face did."

I laugh, accepting the plate he offers. "I'm sorry. That was sexist of me."

"Forgiven. But only because you covered for me this morning." He sits across from me, his long legs briefly bumping mine under the small table. Neither of us moves away. "So, trauma surgery. That's intense."

"Says the man who handled eight different cases single-handedly this morning."

"Different kind of intense." He takes a bite of his sandwich. "What drew you to it?"

"The immediacy," I answer honestly. "No bureaucracy, no committees, just you and the patient and the clock. Either you save them, or you don't."

"Black and white," he notes. "No gray areas."

"Exactly."

"Must be nice." There's no sarcasm in his tone, just genuine reflection. "Out here, everything's gray. Limited resources, patients you've known forever, families depending on your judgment."

I study him across the table, seeing beyond the rugged good looks to the intelligent, committed professional beneath. "How did you end up here? Chicago to Angel's Peak is a big jump."

Something shutters in his expression, but only briefly. "The official version or the truth?"

"The truth, if you're willing to share it."

He sets down his sandwich, considering me. Whatever he sees in my face must reassure him, because he nods slightly before speaking.

"I was engaged to another doctor at Rush. We worked in the ER and had our lives all planned out." His voice is even, but I can hear the careful control in it. "Then she got a once-in-a-lifetime offer to join Doctors Without Borders. Three-year commitment, minimal contact."

"She took it," I guess.

"Didn't even discuss it with me first, just accepted and then presented it as a fait accompli." The hurt is still there, buried but not gone. "She expected me to wait. To put my life on hold while she followed her dream."

"And you weren't willing to do that."

"It wasn't about the waiting," he corrects. "It was about the unilateral decision-making. The assumption that her career took precedence over our relationship." He meets my gaze directly. "Sound familiar, Dr. Department Head?"

It's a direct hit, uncomfortably close to choices I've made myself.

"So you came here to...?"

"To start fresh. Somewhere, I could make my own decisions and have a real impact. Somewhere about as different from Chicago as possible." He smiles wryly. "Mission accomplished on that front."

I digest this, and I understand him better now. His reaction to my comments about my career aspirations and his dedication to this tiny clinic make more sense.

"Do you regret it?" I ask. "Leaving the city?"

"Not for a second." The conviction in his voice is absolute. "The work I do here matters in a way it never could at Rush. These people aren't just cases—they're my community."

Before I can respond, my phone buzzes with an incoming

text. Service must be returning as the roads clear. I check it automatically—then freeze.

"What is it?" Cole asks, noticing my expression.

"The hospital board moved up my final interview. To tomorrow morning." I stare at the screen in disbelief. "If I'm not there, they're giving the position to **Dr. Samuel.**"

"Can't you do it virtually?"

"They specifically say in-person only. It's part of the test— how you handle pressure and unexpected changes." I look up at him, conflicted. "I need to get back to Denver today."

Something flashes in his eyes—disappointment, maybe— but he masks it quickly. "I'll call the sheriff and see if the road to the interstate is open yet."

While he makes the call, I sit there, sandwich forgotten, feeling pulled in two directions. The rational part of me knows I need to get back, that this position represents everything I've worked toward for the past decade. But another part, a part I barely recognize, is strangely reluctant to leave this clinic, this town—this man.

Cole returns, his expression carefully neutral. "Good news and bad news. The road to the interstate should be clear within the hour, but there's another system moving in tonight. If you're going to make it back to Denver, you need to leave as soon as possible."

"Right." I nod, pushing aside my confusion. "I should get my things."

He follows me to the break room, leaning against the doorframe as I gather my bag. The morning's easy camaraderie has evaporated, replaced by a tense awareness that our brief time together is ending.

"I'd offer to drive you to the interstate, but I can't leave the clinic unattended," he says, watching me pack.

"I understand. Really, you've done more than enough already."

When I straighten up, bag in hand, he's closer than I expect. Those blue eyes are intense in a way that makes my pulse quicken.

"Tess," he begins, then stops, seeming to reconsider. "Drive carefully. The roads will still be slick."

"I will." I swing my bag over my shoulder, hyperaware of his proximity in the small room. "Thank you. For everything."

"Just doing my job," he says, but we both know it's been more than that.

We walk to the clinic entrance in silence, and I'm struck by how reluctant I am to walk through that door. It's absurd—I barely know this man and have spent less than twenty-four hours in his company. Yet something significant has happened here, something I can't quite name but can definitely feel.

He hands me a card at the door with the clinic's number scrawled on the back. "In case you run into trouble on the road," he explains. "Cell service is still spotty in places."

"Right. Thank you." I tuck it into my pocket, our fingers brushing in a now-familiar spark of contact.

Before I can overthink it, I rise on tiptoes and press a quick kiss to his cheek. "Goodbye, Cole."

I turn away but he catches my wrist, gentle but firm, spinning me back around. The touch stops me more effectively than if he'd grabbed me with full strength.

"Tess." Just my name, but the way he says it—low and intent—sends a shiver straight through me.

When I meet his eyes, whatever restraint he's been exercising seems to snap. In one fluid motion, he pulls me to him, his free hand coming up to cradle the back of my head as his mouth claims mine.

There's nothing tentative about this kiss. It's confident, commanding, his lips moving against mine with absolute certainty, as if he knows exactly how we fit together. And he does—my body responds instantly, melting against his as my hands find his shoulders, feeling the solid muscle beneath his scrubs.

He angles my head to deepen the kiss, and I open to him willingly, a small sound escaping me as his tongue meets mine. He tastes like coffee and something uniquely him, and I'm suddenly desperate for more, pressing closer as if I could eliminate any space between us.

When he finally pulls back, we're both breathing hard. His eyes have darkened to midnight blue; pupils dilated with the same desire coursing through me.

"That," he says, his voice rough, "is what I wanted to do since you walked through that door yesterday."

I should be shocked by my behavior, by the immediacy and intensity of my response. Instead, I feel only rightness and a burning need for more.

"Cole," I start, not even sure what I'm going to say.

"Go," he interrupts, his thumb brushing my now-swollen bottom lip. "Go to your interview. Get your promotion." His eyes hold mine, unwavering. "But know this isn't finished. Not by a long shot."

The promise in his words—the absolute certainty—sends heat spiraling through me. I swallow hard, trying to regain my composure.

"I'll call you," I say, meaning it despite knowing how unlikely it is that anything could come of this—me in Denver, him here in Angel's Peak.

"Yes," he agrees, as if there's no question about it. "You will."

He steps back, creating distance that feels physically painful, and opens the door for me. Cold air rushes in, a bracing shock after the heat of our exchange.

With one last look at his face—memorizing the strong jaw, those impossible eyes, the mouth that just thoroughly claimed mine—I walk out into the snow-covered parking lot. My car has been cleared, and the path to the road is shoveled. Sometime during the morning, Cole must have did this, preparing for my departure even as we worked side by side.

The thoughtfulness of the gesture breaks my heart and threatens my resolve. It would be so easy to turn around, to walk back into that clinic and into his arms. To see where this unexpected, powerful connection might lead.

Instead, I get into my car and start the engine, watching in the rearview mirror as he stands in the doorway, a tall, solid presence framed by light.

Only when I can no longer see him do I allow myself to touch my lips, still tingling from his kiss, and wonder if I'm driving toward my future or away from it.

Angel's Peak

CHAPTER 3

FIRELIGHT CONFESSIONS

FOUR DAYS. NINETY-SIX HOURS. THAT'S HOW LONG I've been back in Denver, and I still can't get Cole Blake out of my head.

I pace the length of my sleek, modern apartment, phone in hand, staring at his number for what feels like the hundredth time. Outside, another snowstorm rages, not as severe as the one in Angel's Peak but bad enough to make the city lights blur into hazy halos thirty floors below.

The interview went perfectly. Dr. Samuel never stood a chance—I was prepared, polished, and passionate. The board all but confirmed the position is mine; they're just waiting on final approval from the hospital CEO, who's traveling this week.

I should be ecstatic. Instead, I keep replaying that kiss in my mind, feeling the phantom pressure of Cole's lips on mine, his hand cradling my head with that perfect balance of gentleness and command.

"This is ridiculous." I toss my phone onto the couch and walk to the floor-to-ceiling windows.

I barely know the man. One snowed-in night, one

morning working together, one kiss—albeit one hell of a kiss—does not constitute a relationship.

Yet I can't shake the feeling that what happened between us was significant.

Different.

The kind of connection people search years for and rarely find.

My phone buzzes with an incoming text, and I nearly trip over my own feet rushing to check it. Not Cole—just the hospital scheduling office confirming tomorrow's surgeries.

With a frustrated sigh, I grab my tablet and pull up the weather report for Angel's Peak. The storm that hit Denver earlier this week is headed that way, dumping even more snow on the mountain town. I wonder how Cole is managing, if the clinic is busy with weather-related injuries, and if he thinks about me as much as I dream about him.

Before I can talk myself out of it, I dial his number. It rings four times, and I'm about to hang up when he answers.

"Angel's Peak Medical Clinic." His deep and slightly rough voice sends an immediate jolt through me.

"Cole? It's Tess."

A beat of silence, then: "Tess." Just my name, but the way he says it—warmth and surprise and something more—makes my pulse quicken. "I was beginning to think you'd forgotten about me."

"Not likely," I admit, sinking onto my couch. "How are you? I saw you're getting hit with another storm."

"It's pretty bad. Been here since yesterday morning—roads are completely closed again." He sounds tired, but there's a smile in his voice. "How was your interview?"

"Good. Really good, actually. They're just waiting on final approval, but it looks like the position is mine."

"Congratulations, Dr. Carrington. Well-deserved, I'm sure."

"Thank you." An awkward pause follows. There's so much I want to say, yet nothing seems right. How do you tell someone you can't stop thinking about them without sounding desperate or delusional?

Cole breaks the silence. "So, to what do I owe the pleasure of this call? Medical consultation? Weather report? Burning desire to hear my voice?"

I laugh despite myself. "Maybe a little of all three."

"I like that answer." The low timbre of his voice sends warmth flooding through me. "Especially the last part."

Another pause, this one charged with unspoken words.

"I've been thinking about you," I finally admit, closing my eyes. "About that kiss."

"Just the kiss?" The teasing challenge in his tone makes my skin tingle.

"No," I confess. "Not just the kiss."

"Good." His voice drops lower. "Because I've been thinking about a lot more than that. Remembering how you felt pressed against me. Imagining what would have happened if you'd stayed."

My breath catches. The directness of his words, the confident way he expresses his desire without hesitation or apology, is inexplicably arousing.

"Cole," I begin, not even sure what I'm going to say next.

A crash sounds in the background on his end, followed by muffled voices.

"Damn it," he mutters. "Tess, I need to go. Sounds like we have an emergency coming in."

"Of course," I say, professional instinct kicking in. "Go."

"I'll call you back," he promises, and then he's gone.

I stare at my phone, equal parts frustrated and concerned. After a moment's hesitation, I text him: *Let me know if you need any help, medical or otherwise.*

I set my phone aside and try to distract myself with case

files for tomorrow's surgeries. It doesn't work. Every few minutes, I check my phone, wondering what kind of emergency pulled him away, if he's handling it alone, if he's safe.

Two hours later, my phone finally rings.

"Tess?"

"Cole? What happened? Is everything okay?"

"Hey." He sounds exhausted. "Yeah, everyone's okay now. Family of four tried to drive down from their cabin during the storm. Car slid off the road into a snowbank. Nothing serious, just some minor injuries and hypothermia, but they were pretty shaken up."

"Are they still at the clinic?"

"No, I stabilized them and put them into a room at the inn down the street. Roads are still impassable, so they can't get home, but at least they're warm and safe." He sighs heavily. "Sorry about cutting our call short."

"Don't apologize," I say firmly. "It's what we do, right? Emergencies first."

"Right." He's quiet for a moment. "It made me think, though. About how you handled things here at the clinic. Not many specialists would have jumped in like that."

"Just doing my job," I echo his words from days ago.

"No," he corrects me. "You were doing my job. And doing it well." Another pause. "I miss having you here."

The simple admission hits me with unexpected force. "I miss being there," I reply softly.

"Then come back."

"What?" I sit up straighter.

"Come back to Angel's Peak." There's no hesitation in his voice, just that same quiet confidence I remember. "This weekend. The roads should be clear by Friday morning."

"Cole, I—I have surgeries scheduled through Friday afternoon." I'm caught off guard by the directness of his invitation.

"So come Friday night. Or Saturday morning." His tone

softens slightly. "Look, there's something worth exploring between us. Don't tell me you don't feel it."

"I do," I admit, the words slipping out before I can analyze them. "But it's complicated. I'm in Denver, you're there, and with my new position—"

"I'm not asking you to move here," he interrupts gently. "Just come for the weekend. See where this goes. After that, we'll figure it out step by step."

It's the most sensible thing anyone's said to me in a long time. Not grand promises or elaborate plans—just a simple invitation to explore a connection that feels too powerful to ignore.

"Okay," I hear myself say. "I'll come."

"Good." The satisfaction in his voice sends a pleasurable shiver down my spine. "Text me when you're on your way. I'll be waiting."

"Cole," I hesitate, then push forward. "What is this? Between us, I mean."

"I don't know yet," he answers honestly. "But I intend to find out. Don't you?"

When we hang up, I sit motionless for several minutes, replaying the conversation. What am I doing? I haven't had a serious relationship in years, haven't even wanted one with my focus on my career. Now I'm driving back to a mountain town for a man I've known less than a day?

As crazy as it seems, it feels right in a way I can't explain or rationalize. Something is pulling me back to Angel's Peak—to Cole—and for once in my meticulously planned life, I want to follow that pull and see where it leads.

The drive to Angel's Peak on Friday evening is nothing like my harried journey the week before. The roads are clear, the sky a deep, star-filled expanse above the mountains. My car climbs smoothly through the switchbacks, each turn bringing me closer to Cole and whatever awaits us.

I booked a room at Angel's Peak Lodge this time—no need to rely on clinic couches or Jenny's family cabin, though the memory makes me smile. I packed for two nights, telling myself this is just a weekend getaway. A chance to explore the chemistry between us and see if there's anything real beneath the intense attraction.

Though it's well past regular business hours, the clinic lights are still on when I drive through town. I'm tempted to stop, to surprise Cole there, but decide against it. Better to check in at the lodge first and freshen up after the long drive. I text him my arrival and continue up the mountain.

The lodge is everything a mountain retreat should be—a massive stone fireplace in the lobby, exposed wooden beams, and staff dressed in flannel and denim. My room is cozy rather than luxurious, with a king-sized bed covered in a patchwork quilt and windows that will offer mountain views come morning.

I've just emerged from a quick shower when my phone buzzes.

Just finished at the clinic. Can I see you tonight? Or are you too tired from the drive?

I hesitate only briefly before replying: *Not too tired. Come to the lodge?*

His response is immediate: *On my way. 20 minutes.*

Twenty minutes suddenly seems both too long and not long enough. I blow-dry my hair, apply light makeup, and change three times before settling on jeans and a soft blue sweater that brings out my eyes. Casual but not too casual.

At precisely nineteen minutes after his text, there's a knock at my door. My heart hammers against my ribs as I cross the room to answer.

Cole fills the doorway, looking even better than I remember. He's traded scrubs for dark jeans and a charcoal henley that stretches across his broad shoulders. His hair is slightly damp, as if he's just showered, and the scent of his soap mingles with the crisp mountain air clinging to his clothes.

For a long moment, we just look at each other, the week's separation falling away as if it never existed.

"Hi," I finally say, stepping back to let him in.

He enters, bringing with him a presence that immediately makes the room feel smaller. His eyes take me in slowly, appreciatively.

"You look beautiful."

"Thanks." I'm suddenly nervous, unsure of the protocol for whatever this is between us. "How was your day?"

"Long. Better now." He stops in the middle of the room, hands in his pockets, an uncharacteristic hesitation in his stance. "I wasn't sure you'd come."

"Neither was I," I admit, moving to stand before him. "But I couldn't stay away."

Something shifts in his expression, the uncertainty replaced by a focused intent that quickens my pulse. Slowly, deliberately, he raises one hand to cup my cheek, his thumb tracing my lower lip in a gesture that's both tender and possessive.

"I haven't been able to stop thinking about you." His voice drops to that low register that seems to resonate directly in my core. "About that kiss. About what I want to do to you."

The directness of his words sends heat cascading through me. With anyone else, such boldness might seem presumptuous, but from Cole, it feels like a promise my body has been waiting to hear.

"Show me," I whisper, the last coherent words I manage before his mouth claims mine.

Angel's Peak

CHAPTER 4

HEAT AND HUNGER

THIS KISS IS NOTHING LIKE OUR FIRST. WHERE THAT one held surprise and discovery, this one burns with certainty and intent. His lips move against mine with confidence, knowing exactly how much pressure to apply, when to be gentle, and when to demand.

His hands frame my face, holding me steady as he kisses me with a thoroughness that leaves me breathless. I grasp his waist for balance, feeling solid muscle beneath the soft fabric of his shirt.

When he finally pulls back, his eyes are dark, pupils dilated with the same desire coursing through me.

"I've been waiting all week to do that," he murmurs, one hand sliding down to cup the nape of my neck. "To touch you. To taste you."

"Then don't stop," I breathe, rising on tiptoes to press against him.

He laughs softly, the sound rumbling through his chest. "So demanding, Dr. Carrington." His grip tightens slightly, just enough to establish control. "But I think we need to slow down. Talk a little. Make sure we're on the same page."

The restraint he shows, when I can feel how much he wants me pressed against my hip, is strangely more arousing than if he simply swept me to the bed.

"You're right," I concede, though my body protests vehemently.

He reluctantly releases me but keeps one hand lightly on my waist as he glances around the room. "Have you eaten? We could go down to the restaurant."

"Honestly? I'm not hungry." Not for food, anyway.

"No? What are you hungry for?" A slow smile curves his mouth.

"You." The deliberate tease in his tone makes me bold.

Something flares in his eyes, hot and primitive. For a moment, I think he might take me up on my offer, consequences be damned. Then he visibly reins himself in.

"Come." He takes my hand. "Let's go downstairs. Not to the restaurant," he adds when I start to protest. "There's a better place."

Curious, I let him lead me out of the room and down the hall to the elevator. In the enclosed space, his presence feels even more imposing. His clean scent surrounds me. Our shoulders brush, and even that small contact sends electricity skittering across my skin.

Instead of the lobby, he takes us to a lower level I didn't know existed. When the doors open, I understand immediately why he brought me here.

The space is a private lounge, clearly meant for small gatherings or intimate conversations. A massive stone fireplace dominates one wall, a cheerful blaze already burning in the grate. Plush couches and armchairs are arranged around it, with small tables holding hurricane lamps that cast a warm, golden glow over everything.

Best of all, we're completely alone.

"How did you know about this place?" I ask as he leads me toward the fire.

"I grew up coming to this lodge," he explains. "My parents brought us here every winter. This used to be the old game room, but they remodeled a few years back."

"It's beautiful."

"I thought we could talk here," he says, gesturing for me to sit on the couch nearest the fire. "Get to know each other properly, without distractions."

"Without distractions?" I raise an eyebrow, acutely aware of how the firelight accentuates the angles of his face, casting shadows that make him look even more devastating.

He laughs, settling beside me with casual grace. "Well, fewer distractions, anyway."

The couch is smaller than it looks. Our thighs nearly touch. Cole stretches one arm along the back, not quite embracing me but establishing a subtle claim on the space around me.

Perhaps even a claim *on* me.

"So," he begins, his eyes reflecting the dancing flames, "tell me something I don't know about Dr. Tess Carrington."

It's such a simple question, yet it catches me off guard. I'm used to talking about my work, my accomplishments, my goals—not about myself.

"I play the cello," I say finally. "Or I used to, before residency. Haven't touched it in years, but I still have it."

His eyebrows rise in genuine surprise. "Classical training?"

I nod. "Since I was six. My parents thought it would improve my focus and discipline." I smile at the memory. "They weren't wrong."

"I'd like to hear you play someday." There's something in his voice—a quiet certainty that we'll have a 'someday.' *That* makes my chest tighten.

"Your turn," I say, deflecting. "Tell me something I don't know about Cole Blake."

He considers for a moment. "I build furniture. Nothing fancy, just practical pieces. Tables, bookcases. It's meditative, working with my hands in a different way than medicine."

I picture him in a workshop, sleeves rolled up, concentration on his face as he shapes wood into something lasting and useful. The image fits him perfectly.

"Did you make anything in the clinic?" I ask.

"The reception desk. The shelves in the dispensary. The couch you slept on."

"Really?" I'm impressed despite myself. "They're beautiful."

"Thank you." The firelight catches the gold flecks in his blue eyes. "I like creating things that last."

We continue like this, trading small revelations. I learn that he has two older sisters who still live in Chicago, that he broke his arm twice as a kid trying to jump his bike over increasingly ridiculous obstacles, and that he reads military history for relaxation. He learns about my parents' medical practice in Denver, my college year abroad in Spain, and my secret addiction to reality cooking shows.

With each exchange, the sharp edge of my nerves dulls. That anxious buzz that's lived under my skin since he arrived intensifies—turning into something slower. Heavier. A pull I feel low and deep.

But under the comfort, under the steadiness he wraps around me without even trying... desire builds. Steady. Dangerous. It simmers behind the heat in his gaze, in the way he watches my mouth when I speak, like he's already imagining what he'll do to silence it.

He brushes my hair back. Fingers trail along my arm, light and unhurried, like he's taking inventory. Then—his thumb finds the inside of my wrist. Slow. Intentional. Tracing the thrum of my pulse like it belongs to him.

A shiver rolls through me, sharp and unbidden.

"Cold?" he asks, but the glint in his eye says he knows better.

"No," I admit softly, eyes flicking up to meet his. "Not cold."

His gaze darkens, heat and intention blooming there, and suddenly, the air between us crackles.

He turns then, his full focus locked on me. One hand slides from the back of the couch to the side of my neck. Not rough—but firm. Certain. Fingers splayed beneath my jaw, his thumb pressing lightly just under my ear.

"Tess." My name from his lips is low. Reverent. A sin and a promise. "I need you to hear me."

My breath hitches. The part of me that always expects rejection braces.

Here it comes.

He's taken. He's not interested. He's not looking for anything.

I brace myself for disappointment, but that's not what this is.

"I want you," he says, voice steady. "Badly. Have from the second you walked into my clinic. Before we go any further..." His thumb glides down my throat, pausing in the dip where my pulse pounds like a warning. Or a welcome.

A pause. Intentional. Weighted.

"I'm not soft. I don't move slow. I take what I want. I love hard. I fuck harder." His gaze dips to my mouth and lingers. "I don't pretend to be anything less than what I am."

I forget how to breathe.

His thumb traces a slow, burning path down the side of my throat, pausing at the hollow where my pulse pounds wildly beneath the skin.

"Some women," he continues, voice dropping into a darker register, rougher, hungrier, "hear the warning, and they bolt. And that's fine." He shifts closer, crowding me just enough that the air between us turns molten. His fingers flex against my skin. "But others..." His eyes flick back to mine, and the heat there steals whatever will I had left. "They burn for me."

My thighs press together, instinctive and useless. I go still, the truth of his words sinking in, lighting me up from the inside.

"I want to make *you* burn." His voice dips lower, turning to smoke and heat. His mouth hovers close, but he doesn't kiss me. He waits. Letting me feel the weight of his words.

The inevitability of *him*.

He's a man who wants ruin.

"I want to be clear. Once I start, I won't stop until I've had every part of you."

My pulse stutters. He hasn't even kissed me, and already I feel unraveled—peeling open under the heat of his voice alone.

I swallow hard. "What does that mean... to burn for you?"

"Enough to scare some women away." He leans in, just enough that his breath brushes my lips—warm, deliberate, unmistakably in control. "Enough to draw others like moths to a flame." His gaze pins me, dark and unrelenting. "So tell me..." His voice is a low rasp now, intimate and commanding. "Are you willing to burn for me? Or are you going to hear my warning and run?"

A pause follows, thick and taut, heavy with everything he refuses to soften for my comfort.

I swallow, pulse racing, throat dry.

"That depends."

His brow lifts, just barely. "On what?"

I hold his gaze, even though my heart thuds against my ribs.

"Are we talking shades of gray?" I let the words hang for a beat, then finish. For a second, he's completely still.

Then—a wicked, low laugh, the sound rolling through him like thunder that knows exactly where it's striking.

"Darker," he says, voice rough with promise. "Much darker. The kind you don't read about in glossy paperbacks with safe words printed in bold."

His hand tightens ever so slightly on my neck—not to control me, but to steady me.

"Still want to play with fire, sweetheart?"

A week ago, I would've laughed at the question. Me, surrender control? Impossible.

But with Cole—this man who radiates certainty, who sees past the armor I wear like glass—I want to know what it feels like to let go.

To let him lead.

And maybe, just maybe... to *burn* for him.

"Make me burn," I whisper, the word falling from my lips like a confession.

Something flares in his eyes—satisfaction, desire, and something deeper I can't quite name. His hand tightens slightly on my neck, thumb pressing gently against my racing pulse.

"I knew you wouldn't run," he murmurs.

The words hit something primal. Something buried. Something that aches to surrender—not because I'm weak, but because for once... I don't have to be strong.

My voice is a breath. "Light the match, Cole."

His smile is slow. Dangerous. Triumphant.

"Gladly."

And then he kisses me.

Not tentative. Not testing.

Claiming.

His mouth crashes into mine with the kind of force that

should bruise but doesn't. Because somehow, even now, he holds back just enough.

One hand fists in my hair, angling my face to meet him the way he wants. The other stays wrapped around the side of my neck, grounding me. His lips move over mine like he's tasting something he's been craving for far too long—hungry but in control.

Deep.

Demanding.

Like he's carving the memory of this moment into bone.

I gasp against his mouth, and he takes that, too—tongue sliding past my lips like he has every right to it.

He tastes like heat and danger, something I've never had before, and something I won't be able to live without.

He doesn't pull away. Doesn't pause. Doesn't give me time to think.

He devours.

And I let him.

I want to let him.

My hands find the hard line of his chest, fingers curling into his shirt, needing more even as my body lights up like I've been plugged into a live wire.

The kiss turns darker. Deeper. Dirtier.

His grip tightens in my hair just enough to make me gasp again.

"I knew it," he growls against my lips, voice rough with satisfaction. "You were made for me."

For him.

I'm already burning.

And I never want it to stop.

His free hand slides to my waist, then lower, pulling me firmly against him until I'm half in his lap. I should feel ridiculous—thirty-two years old, making out on a couch like a teenager—but all I feel is a burning need for more of him, more of this.

"Cole," I gasp when he finally releases my mouth to trail kisses down my neck. "There could be people—"

"There won't be," he murmurs, nipping gently at my earlobe. "Lodge manager is a friend. This room is ours for the night."

The implication that he planned this—secured this space in anticipation of our reunion—sends a fresh wave of heat through me. Instead of feeling manipulated, I feel seen. Cared for. Desired.

His mouth finds that sensitive spot just below my ear, and I moan, my fingers digging into his shoulders.

"Like that?" he whispers against my skin, and when I nod, he does it again—slower. "Tell me what you want. I need to hear you say it."

The demand pulls me from the haze. It would be easy to give him something vague. But this man? He deserves more than vague.

"I want you to take me," I say, voice steady. "I want to feel your hands on me. Your mouth. All of you."

His smile is devastating—tender and predatory all at once.

"And then? What else do you want?"

I meet his eyes without flinching. "I want you inside me." A breath. A heartbeat. "I want you to make me yours."

His breath hitches. I've hit something deep.

But I'm not done.

I slide my hand to his jaw, forcing him to see me.

"To be what you need." My voice is low, but there's no mistaking the conviction.

His eyes go molten.

"*Fuuuuck*," he breathes, the rare profanity revealing just how affected he is. "You have no idea what you do to me when you talk like that."

He doesn't move, doesn't breathe—just stares at me like I've undone something inside him.

Then he exhales, rough and reverent.

"Jesus, Tess."

His mouth crashes into mine, and this time?

There's no restraint.

Only fire.

His hands slide to the hem of my sweater—no hesitation, no request. Just claiming.

He lifts it slowly, dragging the fabric up my torso, over my ribs, higher—each inch baring skin kissed golden by the flickering firelight. When it clears my head, he tosses it aside without looking, his eyes locked on me like I've become the only thing he sees.

He leans back just enough to take me in.

His eyes darken. Jaw flexes.

Possession settles into him like instinct.

"Look at you," he murmurs. Low. Rough. Reverent. "All mine."

I move toward him, heart pounding, body already swaying toward the gravity of his, but—

"Stand."

One word. A command.

It lands between my legs like a spark to dry tinder.

I rise. Unsteady at first, breath shallow. But his gaze holds me upright, centers me in a way that feels both terrifying and safe.

He stays seated. Legs spread slightly, hands resting on his thighs, fingers flexing just once as his gaze rakes down my body.

Like he's starving. Like he's already decided how he's going to consume me.

"Now…" His voice is silk stretched tight over steel. "The jeans."

I reach for the button. My fingers tremble, but I don't look away from him.

"Slowly."

The word is soft. Dangerous.

I pull the zipper down. The sound feels impossibly loud in the charged silence between us.

"Eyes on me." Another command.

I hook my thumbs into the waistband, dragging the denim down my hips, inch by inch.

His eyes never leave mine. Not once.

He watches me watch him.

I've never felt more exposed. More wanted. More desired.

I step out of the jeans, firelight catching on bare skin and pale blue lace. My pulse thuds in my ears, heat licking up my spine.

"Bra," he says simply.

I reach back, hands moving to the clasp—

"Don't."

The single syllable stills me.

His gaze drops to my chest, then back to my face.

"Leave it," he says, voice low and guttural. "I like the way it looks on you."

A beat passes. Tension coils tight.

Then—

"Panties."

Angel's Peak

CHAPTER 5

NO GOING BACK

I SHOULDN'T CRAVE THE SOUND OF A COMMAND.

Shouldn't want to obey.

But when Cole tells me to take off my panties, I don't hesitate.

I can't.

My body moves before my mind catches up—driven not by fear but by something darker. Deeper.

A need I've never acknowledged, let alone acted on.

This is the first time I've ever let a man take control.

Not just of my body.

Of me.

And instead of shame, I feel... *free*.

Weightless. Exposed in a way that doesn't scare me—not with him.

Because his voice?

It's the spark and the fuse.

The lock and the key.

The anchor I never knew I needed.

I hook my thumbs into the lace and begin to lower them—

"Eyes on me." The command slices through the haze like lightning.

I lift my gaze to his, and the moment our eyes lock, it happens—

I fall.

Not away. Not apart.

Into him.

I swallow hard, sliding them down slowly, aware of how exposed I am, how much power he's taken—and how much I've given.

When I'm bare before him, he leans forward, one hand reaching out to skim the outside of my thigh, the barest graze of knuckles.

"Perfect," he murmurs. "Every inch of you. And now that you've undressed for me, sweetheart..."

He looks up at me with eyes full of heat and possession.

"I'm going to take my time making you forget how to breathe."

He pulls his henley over his head, revealing a body that makes my breath catch. Broad shoulders, thick with strength, taper down to a narrow waist. Ropes of lean muscle shift beneath golden skin, a dusting of dark hair trailing down his chest, disappearing beneath the waistband of his jeans.

I stare, helpless to hide it.

"Like what you see?" he asks, smug and dark with amusement.

I reach for him, fingertips grazing the heat of his chest, tracing the ridges of muscle and the line of his sternum.

He lets me touch—for a moment.

Then he captures my wrists in one firm hand, stilling me with nothing more than strength and a low command:

"My turn."

My pulse spikes.

"Lie back."

The words leave no room for argument. My body obeys before my brain catches up, sinking into the cushions, heart hammering.

He shifts over me slowly, deliberately—his weight caging me in. Not trapping. *Claiming*. One hand braced beside my head, the other free.

His mouth finds my ear. Breath hot. Close enough to feel but not kiss.

Teasing.

Torturing.

"Do you have any idea," he murmurs, voice low and frayed, "how many nights I've imagined you like this?" His hips press between my thighs. Hard. Heavy. Unmistakably ready. "Beneath me. Needing me. Arching. Gasping." A pause. His voice dips lower, darker. "Begging to be filled. To be fucked?"

A moan slips from my throat, broken and involuntary.

His lips drag just beneath my ear, tracing fire along my skin.

"I've jerked off thinking about this," he growls. "So many fucking times I lost count."

Each word is sharp. Ripped from somewhere deep.

"Fisting my cock to the thought of you writhing under me, whimpering my name. Coming so hard your legs shake while I keep you wide open and begging for more."

I arch, breath shattered.

He groans against my neck, the sound guttural, like my reaction feeds something primal inside him.

"Every time," he says, voice hoarse. "Every single time, I told myself the real thing would wreck me." His hand slides down my ribs, not soft—sure. "And fuck, Tess..." His mouth claims mine in a kiss that's all teeth and heat and hunger. "...I was right."

A growl rumbles in his chest. He claims my mouth again,

deeper this time, hungrier, more demanding. My bra loosens with a flick of his fingers, sliding down my arms as he pulls it away like wrapping off a gift.

I resist the urge to cover myself—bare, exposed—under the full weight of his gaze.

His eyes flare.

"Perfect," he murmurs, possessive and reverent. He palms one breast, rough fingers teasing as his mouth closes around the other, tongue circling, then sucking hard enough to make me cry out.

"That's it." His voice is thick. Commanding. "Let me hear you. Let me know exactly what I'm doing to you."

My nails dig into the couch. I can't hold back. Not from him.

His hand trails lower, slow and deliberate, fingertips brushing my abdomen, making my muscles jump. When he reaches my hip, he doesn't ask.

He just waits.

The silence between us grows heavy, charged—a question without words.

And I answer it.

"I want... I want to feel you." My voice is barely a whisper. "I want your hands on me. I want you to take me."

His hand stills, just for a second.

"Slow and soft?" he asks, voice a low murmur, dark and coaxing. "Or fast and hard?"

My breath hitches. I know what he's doing—testing me. Giving me a choice before he takes the rest.

"As hard as you need." I meet his gaze. I swallow. "I want to feel you."

My words detonate something between us.

His eyes darken like a storm rolling in.

"That's my girl." His hand slides behind my neck. He fists

my hair as he leans in, his voice brushing my skin like a kiss. "Hands above your head."

My heart stutters.

He waits. Watching.

I obey.

"Keep them there. You move, I stop. Understood?"

"Yes." My voice trembles.

He tilts his head. "Yes, what?"

I blink, confused, mouth parting. "What do you mean?"

His grip tightens, a slow smile curving his lips as he whispers in my ear.

"When we're like this, I want you to call me Sir."

The words slam through me, hot and electric.

Not just because of what they mean—but because of how it feels.

I'm a woman who's used to control, to clinical precision, to being in charge. Saying *Sir*—especially during sex—feels foreign on my tongue, like stepping into a version of myself I've never allowed before.

It should feel awkward. Embarrassing.

But instead, it feels like heat crawling up my spine.

Sir.

The syllable lands in my mouth like something forbidden —foreign, intimate, and laced with power.

Not his power. *Mine.*

Because I'm the one giving it. Offering it.

I pause and then breathe it out, excitement curling in my belly like a fuse lit at both ends.

"Yes... Sir?" It feels like I've just handed him the reins to my body and my soul. And God help me, the look on his face when I say it?

The triumphant expression he gives me is pure sin, full of dark promise. His fingers slide through slick heat, deliberate and unhurried, parting me with the kind of precision that says he already knows exactly how I'll come apart.

The weight of control slips off my shoulders, landing square on him, leaving me with pure, visceral sensation.

"Christ," he mutters, voice low, reverent, ruined. "You're soaked for me already. You like giving up control that much?"

My breath catches. My hips jerk against his hand, but I don't drop my arms.

"I've never..." The words snag in my throat, fragile and raw. "I've never done anything like this before."

His hand stills. Just for a second.

Then his gaze locks onto mine—dark, intense, completely focused.

"No one's ever taken control like this?"

"No." I shake my head.

"No one's ever made you call them Sir?"

"No..." And then I remember. "No, sir." Another shake. Barely a breath.

"No one's ever bound you with their voice and made you beg?"

The flush rises fast—neck to cheeks, shame and excitement tangled so tight I can't tell them apart.

"No, sir," I whisper.

A beat of silence.

Then—

"Fuck."

The word is rough, reverent.

His forehead drops to mine, and for a second, he breathes me in.

"Good," he says finally, voice like gravel and smoke. "Because that means I get to be your first." His grip tightens in my hair, and his other hand resumes its slow, merciless exploration. "Your first and last surrender."

Last?

My head tips back, lips parting on a gasp.

"And sweetheart?" His mouth finds my throat, open and hot. "It's gonna ruin you for anything less."

He presses the heel of his palm against my clit, grinding slow, devastating circles. His other hand grips my hip tight, holding me perfectly still.

I try to move—just a little.

He stops.

"What did I say?"

My eyes fly open. "Don't move."

"Good girl."

When he touches me again—the press of his fingers against my center sends a jolt through me. My hips buck involuntarily. He chuckles, the sound dark and satisfied, as he strokes me with deliberate skill.

"So responsive," he murmurs, watching my face as he circles the bundle of nerves at my core. "So perfect for me."

His touch is exquisite—confident without being rough, knowing without being mechanical. He reads my reactions with the same intuitive understanding I've seen him apply to his patients, adjusting pressure and rhythm based on the catch in my breath and the tension in my muscles.

When he slides one finger inside me, then two, I moan his name, beyond caring about our semi-public location. The building pleasure is too intense and consuming to allow for such mundane concerns.

"That's it," he encourages, crooking his fingers to find the spot that makes me see stars. "Let go for me. Let me watch you come apart."

His thumb circles my clit in time with the thrust of his fingers, and the dual sensation sends me spiraling toward a precipice I didn't know could be reached so quickly. When he lowers his head to take one nipple between his teeth, applying just enough pressure to skirt the edge of pain, I shatter completely.

The orgasm crashes through me in waves, my body arching off the couch as I cry out his name. He works me through it, gentling his touch but not stopping until the last tremor subsides and I collapse boneless against the cushions.

"Beautiful." He kisses my collarbone softly as I struggle to catch my breath. "So fucking beautiful when you come for me."

I've never felt anything like it—not just the blinding rush of release, but the obliteration of everything I thought I had to be.

For those moments, I wasn't Dr. Tess Carrington with all her sharp edges and perfectly stacked ambitions. I was just a woman—his woman—undone beneath his hands, stripped bare in every way that matters.

Raw. Real. Completely his.

As my awareness returns, so does the press of him—thick, hard, unrelenting—still pulsing against my thigh like a promise he hasn't yet made good on.

I reach for him, instinctive and aching to give something back.

But his hand snaps around my wrist—not rough, but unyielding.

His grip stops me cold.

"No."

The word lands like a slap of heat, sharp and immediate.

His eyes flash, dark and uncompromising as he leans in.

"You don't get to touch me like that."

My breath catches.

"You don't take from me." His voice is low, commanding. "That's my job. My hands. My mouth. My body—they're yours, but only when I give them to you."

He brings my hand to his lips, brushing a kiss across my knuckles with a softness that contrasts the steel in his tone.

But I see it now. Feel it.

That softness? It's not permission. It's the calm before the storm.

"Don't reach for control," he murmurs against my skin. "You won't find it."

He lets my hand go slowly, deliberately. His gaze never wavers.

"You're going to learn how good it feels to let me take care of you." A slow, satisfied smile curves his lips. "How amazing it feels to obey..."

The last of my breath leaves in a shudder.

"As for fucking you. Not here." His voice is wrecked with restraint. Barely leashed hunger coils beneath every word. "Not like this."

"But—"

"When I take you..." His voice cuts through the room like a blade. Low. Unapologetic. Possessive. "I'm going to spread you out in a real bed and taste every inch of your skin. I'm going to fuck you so deep and so slow you'll forget your name before I let you come again." He holds my gaze. Doesn't blink. Doesn't waver. "...I'm going to wreck you."

My breath leaves me in a rush.

"I've waited too long to rush this. And when I slide inside you, I want your legs wrapped around me. I want your nails clawing my back. I want to feel every tremble when you break for me again and again."

His hand trails down my ribs, over my bare stomach. Just a brush. A warning.

"This isn't going to be quick and dirty." His voice drips with molten steel. "I'm going to take all night to fuck you."

The heat that sparks low in my belly reignites like gasoline to flame.

I look up at him, flushed, trembling, already half wrecked and desperate for more.

"Then take me to bed," I whisper, every word soaked in need. "Take me upstairs."

He studies me. Not with uncertainty—but with precision.

Still. Silent. Waiting.

The air thickens, charged and heavy.

His gaze doesn't flicker. Doesn't soften.

And that's when I realize—he's waiting for my submission.

My pulse stutters.

Heat floods my chest.

He's giving me the choice—but only once.

A beat of silence stretches between us, thick with expectation.

Then I exhale, shaky and sure all at once.

"Please, take me upstairs... Sir."

The shift is instant.

His eyes darken like smoke swallowing fire. His jaw tightens. A slow, dark smile curls across his lips.

"There she is." He steps forward, towering, consuming me. "My sweet submissive."

His voice is all command now. Smooth. Cold fire.

"Get dressed." He bends, retrieves my sweater from the floor, and hands it to me without looking away.

Every nerve in my body hums with anticipation.

Whatever he sees on my face must satisfy him. Because his expression shifts—dark, decisive.

I feel his hunger. Every word of it.

In every inch of my still-burning skin.

As I readjust my clothing with trembling fingers, he banks the flames, his movements efficient and practiced. The firelight plays across his muscular back, highlighting strength contained in grace, power held in check.

He returns to me only when I'm fully dressed, extending a hand to help me up from the couch. The simple courtesy, after the intimate moments we've just shared, touches me deeply.

"Ready?" he asks, and though the question is simple, I hear the layers beneath it.

Ready for more physical pleasure? *Yes.*

Ready for whatever this connection between us might become, whatever path we're starting down together? *I think so.*

"Yes, sir." I place my hand in his, feeling the strength in his grip, the sureness in his touch.

Hand in hand, we walk toward the elevator, leaving the dying embers behind us and moving toward a fire of our own making.

Angel's Peak

Chapter 6

Mountain Morning

I wake to sunlight streaming through unfamiliar curtains and the solid weight of an arm draped across my waist. For a moment, I'm disoriented, my brain struggling to reconcile the rustic wooden beams above me with my sleek Denver apartment.

Then Cole shifts beside me, his warmth pressed along the length of my back, and memories of last night flood through me in a heated rush.

The elevator ride to my room, his mouth never leaving mine. The door barely closed before clothes were discarded. His body, even more magnificent than I imagined, moving over mine. Claiming me. His voice, rough with desire, telling me exactly what he wanted to do to me—and then doing it with devastating precision.

I flush at the recollection of how completely I surrendered, how eagerly I followed his commands. I've never experienced anything like it—the freedom that came with letting go, with putting myself entirely in his capable hands.

"I can hear you thinking," Cole murmurs, his voice morning-rough against my ear. His arm tightens around me, pulling me more firmly against him. "Having regrets, Dr. Carrington?"

I turn in his embrace to face him, drinking in the sight of him in the morning light. His hair is tousled from sleep, and my fingers, stubble darkening his jaw, eyes still heavy-lidded. He looks different somehow—more brutally handsome—and the intimacy of waking together softens the intensity I associate with him.

"No regrets," I assure him, tracing the line of his collarbone with one finger. "Just... processing."

"Processing what, exactly?" He captures my wandering hand, bringing it to his lips for a kiss that sends a shiver of remembered pleasure through me.

"Surrendering control." I consider how to explain the tangle of thoughts and feelings his touch has awakened in me. "I'm not like that."

"And yet you surrendered beautifully." His eyes darken with remembered heat. "For me."

"Yes. For you," I agree softly.

He shifts, propping himself on one elbow to look down at me more directly. His free hand cups my cheek, thumb tracing my lower lip in a gesture that's already become familiar.

"Does that bother you?"

I consider the question honestly. Does it bother me that this man I barely know unearthed a side of myself I don't recognize? That he commanded my body with an authority I've never permitted anyone before?

"No," I realize with some surprise. "It doesn't bother me at all. It... excites me."

His slow smile is equal parts tenderness and masculine satisfaction. "Good. Because watching you let go, seeing you trust me enough to surrender—" He shakes his head as if words are inadequate. "It was the most beautiful thing I've ever seen."

Something warm unfurls in my chest at his words, something that feels dangerously like more than physical attraction or the afterglow of exceptional sex.

Before I can examine the feeling too closely, Cole's mouth finds mine in a kiss that starts gentle but quickly deepens, his body shifting to cover mine. I open to him willingly, arms winding around his neck as his weight settles perfectly between my thighs.

"Good morning," he murmurs against my lips, his arousal pressing hard against my hip.

"Good morning, *Sir*," I whisper back, voice breathy but sure—an offering and a challenge wrapped in one.

He stills for a beat. Then lifts his head, eyes locking onto mine with that slow-burning intensity that makes my pulse skip.

"Say that again."

"Good morning, Sir." My lips part, heat blooming in my cheeks.

The shift in him is instant. The lazy affection of waking together tightens into something darker, more deliberate.

"Arms above your head," he orders, voice low but firm. "Now."

I obey without hesitation, stretching out beneath him, the sheets cool against my bare skin as my wrists fall into place above the pillows.

His eyes rake over me with open hunger, satisfaction curling at the corners of his mouth like he's admiring a masterpiece he fully intends to wreck.

"That's better."

He traces a line down my throat, slow and claiming, before leaning in to whisper against my skin.

"Let's see how deep your trust goes, sweetheart."

His mouth returns to my breast, tongue circling before he sucks hard enough to make me gasp.

"Keep those hands where they are," he growls. "You move them without permission. You don't get to come."

The words strike like a match against already-burning skin.

I lie beneath him, exposed and trembling, arms pinned above my head by my own obedience. The air between us tightens, heavy with expectation. With control.

With power—his, not mine.

Cole watches me like a man on the edge of restraint, eyes raking over my body as though he's memorizing every inch he owns. He shifts lower, mouth hot and unrelenting against my breast, then he trails kisses down my ribcage, each one sharper, wetter, rougher than the last. There's no pretense of gentleness now—only hunger.

Possession.

Command.

He lifts off me only long enough to flip me. One hard motion, and I'm on my stomach, breath stolen from my lungs as the mattress dips beneath his weight.

"Stay there," he growls, pressing his hand between my shoulder blades to keep me down. The dominance in his voice isn't playful—it's absolute.

His other hand slides down the length of my back, fingers following the curve of my spine before gripping my hip, dragging me back into alignment with him.

He doesn't ask. He takes.

"This is all mine now," he mutters, voice rough and full of wicked reverence.

He rocks against me, his arousal an unspoken promise— hard, relentless, and utterly in control.

When he presses forward, I gasp into the sheets. It's deeper like this. Rougher. Every movement slams into me with intent, with force, and with the kind of dominance that sears itself into my memory.

"Take it," he snarls. "Take everything I give you."

I do. Because I want it. I want him. All of him.

And he doesn't hold back.

He pulls me up by the shoulders, chest against my back, hand threading into my hair to keep my head tilted where he wants it.

"Look at you," he breathes into my ear. "My cock buried in your pussy. You were made for this." He pulls out and then slams forward, making me gasp. "For me."

I cry out—raw, aching. Not in pain, but in surrender.

And still, he doesn't relent. He shifts again, manhandling me onto my back, dragging my body to the edge of the bed like it's nothing, his mouth claiming mine in a brutal, consuming kiss that tastes like fire and freedom.

"Tell me who you belong to," he demands between kisses.

"You," I gasp. "I belong to you."

"Say it right."

I lock eyes with him. Let him see what he's done to me.

"I belong to you, Sir."

That breaks him.

He drives into me again, deeper, rougher, every thrust a declaration, a marking of territory until the only sounds in the room are gasps, groans, and the desperate rhythm of bodies colliding.

My arms strain. My back arches. My vision blurs.

"You take me so well," he growls, voice ragged. "Like you were made for me."

I shatter for him. Again. And again.

And when he finally falls with me, body pressed full-length to mine, breath ragged in my ear, I feel the shift. The rawness between us has morphed into something else.

Something dangerous. Something real.

Something that feels like *more*.

The day disappears in shadows and sweat, time unraveling

in the hush of my room, in the rough cadence of our breath, in the endless press of skin on skin.

Cole doesn't relent.

He claims me in every way a man can—on the bed, against the wall, under the steaming spray of the shower, where his hands slide over slick skin and whispered orders melt into moans.

He introduces restraints with quiet authority, tethering me to his will, his rhythm.

A blindfold follows—the velvet darkness heightens every sound and sensation, making me tremble before he even touches me.

Sometimes, he takes me slowly, with reverent patience that leaves me aching for more.

Sometimes, he's ruthless, his voice the only thing anchoring me, calling me back from the edge again and again.

When I think I have nothing left to give, he shows me I've only just begun to yield to him.

Outside, the sky shifts from the brilliant blue of day to starry midnight black. We spend the entire day in the room—and the night that follows—lost in sweat and shadows, tangled sheets and whispered sins.

On Sunday, I wake to the dusky gray just before dawn, my body beautifully bruised and thoroughly used.

He touches me like a man claiming something. Again. And again. Until all that's left of me is heat and obedience.

Now, I kneel between his legs, muscles sore, mind blissfully empty.

He sits at the edge of the bed, shirtless, sweat-slicked, gloriously unhurried. One hand wraps around the base of his cock. The other sinks into my hair, gripping tight.

He guides me down onto his cock with slow, deliberate pressure. I follow without hesitation.

Not because he forces me.

Because every cell in my body aches to please him.

He watches me with half-lidded eyes. A king on his throne.

I've never felt more wrecked. Or more willing.

His voice is rough silk, frayed and filthy.

"Look at you," he murmurs, thumb brushing over my cheekbone, tender in contrast to the relentless grip in my hair. "On your knees for me. My cock in your mouth. God, you're stunning."

I would answer if I could, but the only sound I manage is a soft whimper, needy and reverent.

Then—

The shrill cry of my phone slices through the moment.

Cole stills, his whole body going tense. A low, guttural groan escapes through clenched teeth.

"Tell me that's not your phone."

I freeze, shame and frustration crashing over me in the same wave. My body still humming from the power of his touch, from serving him, but reality has to ruin the moment.

My forehead drops to his thigh, and I breathe through the ache—both physical and emotional.

"I have to check," I whisper. "It could be an emergency."

He doesn't move for a beat. Then, with a sigh that's half restraint, half resignation, he loosens his grip in my hair and gently nudges me back.

"Go ahead," he says, rolling away to give me space.

I reach blindly for the nightstand, fingers closing around my phone. The screen blinks with a name I can't ignore.

"It's the hospital," I murmur, dread knotting in my stomach. Responsibility wraps around me like a second skin, even as the warmth of him lingers on my tongue.

I swipe to answer.

"Tess, thank God," comes Dr. Patel's tense voice. "We've got a situation. Major pileup on I-70. Multiple trauma victims, two with complex vascular injuries—my cases—but I'm stuck in Chicago. Canceled flight."

As he talks, I feel the shift. My mind sharpens. My body resets. Adrenaline replacing arousal.

Back in the world. Back in the work.

"They're stable for now," he finishes, "but we need you. No one else has your experience with this type of injury pattern."

I glance at Cole. He's already watching me, calm but knowing.

He already knows what I'm about to say.

"I'll be there as soon as I can," I reply. "Four hours. Less if traffic cooperates."

"Thank you. OR team's prepping for your arrival."

The call ends. Silence stretches for a heartbeat. Then Cole is already moving, gathering my clothes with a quiet efficiency that tells me he's been in situations like this too many times to waste breath on protest.

"You have to go."

"I do."

I run a hand through my tangled hair, already calculating routes, ETA, and possible surgical plans.

"Vascular trauma. Patel's stuck. I'm the fallback."

Cole nods, handing me my jeans, like we're suiting up for battle in separate wars. "How long will the surgery take?"

"Five or six hours minimum. Could be longer."

"So you won't be back."

The regret in his voice cuts deeper than I expect.

"No."

I stand, reaching for my bra, but pause. Something twists in my chest—not guilt. Not exactly. It's something sharper. Something that feels like loss before it even has a chance to become anything more.

He watches me quietly.

"I'll make you coffee." He reaches for his jeans. "You shouldn't drive back to Denver on an empty stomach."

I step toward him and press a hand to his chest, halting him mid-motion.

"I don't need coffee," I murmur, eyes locked on his. "And there's still time... for this."

My gaze drops deliberately to the thick line of his arousal straining behind his jeans.

Then I look up again. Open. Unashamed.

"You started something," I whisper, lips parted, voice laced with reverence and hunger. "Use me." A breath. A heartbeat. "Let me serve you. One last time... before I go."

His breath hitches. His entire body goes still—like he's afraid to move and break the spell. The silence between us tightens.

His jaw flexes.

And just like that—his control snaps into place, sharp and absolute.

His hand finds my hair. The other brushes the curve of my jaw.

"On your knees, sweetheart." His eyes go dark. Lethal. Possessive.

And I drop to my knees.

His hand slides into my hair, curling tight—not painful, but commanding. Grounding. His hips shift forward, pressing against my mouth in silent expectation. The look he gives me steals my breath.

"Open for me, sweetheart." His voice is velvet-wrapped sin. "Take me deep."

And I do.

Lips parting. Heart racing.

Knees pressed to the hardwood.

Every nerve alive and aching for him.

I take him slowly, deliberately, tongue tracing the length of him as he groans low and curses under his breath.

"Fuck... Tess."

I hollow my cheeks, watching the effect I have on him—the way his breath stutters, his thighs tense, his control frays with every stroke.

For the first time all morning... He's the one unraveling.

Angel's Peak

Chapter 7

The Edge of Goodbye

I take him into my mouth with the same hunger I felt all night, with the same desire to give, to worship, to burn this moment into both of us.

He groans low, hips tightening under my grip, and his free hand braces on the wall behind him.

"God that's good…" The words leave him ragged. "Just like that."

I give him everything—my mouth, my obedience, my farewell.

By the time he comes undone, shuddering and whispering my name like a prayer, I've left a mark on him.

Just as he's left one on me.

Twenty minutes later, we're in the lodge's restaurant, which is just opening for breakfast. Cole speaks briefly to the hostess—someone he knows, given her familiar smile—and we're led to a quiet corner table with a view of the mountains.

"Perks of being the town's medical provider," he explains as coffee appears almost immediately. "Everyone wants to stay on your good side."

"Smart of them," I say, doctoring my coffee with cream. "Especially when the provider is as competent as you."

He inclines his head at the compliment but doesn't dwell on it. Instead, he watches me with those perceptive blue eyes that seem to see more than I intend to reveal.

"You're already gone," he observes after a moment. "Mentally, I mean. You're already in that OR."

I start to deny it, then realize he's right. Part of my mind is already walking through the procedures I'll need to perform, anticipating complications, and preparing for the intense focus that trauma surgery demands.

"I'm sorry. It's how I operate," I admit, then smile at the unintentional pun. "Literally and figuratively. I need to prepare mentally."

"I understand." And he does. This is another area where our differences in specialty don't extend to our fundamental approach to medicine. "It's one of the things I admire about you."

The simple statement catches me off guard. "You hardly know me," I remind him.

"I know enough." His hand covers mine on the table, warm and steady. "I know you're brilliant at what you do. I know you care deeply about your patients, even the ones you haven't met yet. I know you're willing to drop everything and drive four hours to perform surgery that few others can handle."

Put that way, it does sound like he knows significant things about me—the things that matter professionally, at least.

"And I know," he continues, his voice dropping lower, "that last night wasn't just physical for either of us. I'm not giving that up."

The waitress arrives with our food—simple but hearty breakfast plates that would typically make my mouth water.

Today, I'm too distracted by Cole's words, by the intensity in his gaze, to appreciate the perfect omelet before me.

"I feel it too," I admit quietly once we're alone again. "But, my life is in Denver. My career is there. This position I'm about to get—it's everything I've worked for."

"I'm not asking you to give any of that up," he says, his tone reasonable. "I'm just asking for a chance to see what this could be."

"Long distance rarely works," I point out, picking at my food.

"It does when both people want it to." He takes a bite of his breakfast, chewing thoughtfully before continuing. "Look, I'm not saying it would be easy. Denver is three hours away in good weather and four in bad. We both have demanding jobs with unpredictable schedules. But if what I felt with you last night—what I'm feeling right now—is even a fraction of what's possible between us, it's worth the effort."

His directness is both refreshing and unsettling. Most men I've dated would be hedging by now, backing away from anything that resembled commitment after what essentially amounts to a one-night stand. But Cole isn't most men, as I've been discovering since we met.

"I don't know if I can do casual," I tell him honestly. "Not with my schedule, not with the demands of this new position."

"Who said anything about casual?" He leans forward, eyes intent on mine. "I don't do casual either. Not in my work, not in my life, and definitely not with you."

The echo of his words from last night—about how he needs to be in control—sends a shiver of awareness through me. He's applying the same intensity, the same absolute certainty, to the possibility of a relationship that he brought to our physical connection.

"What are you saying, exactly?" I ask, needing clarity.

"I'm saying I want to see you again. Regularly. Exclusively." His directness leaves no room for misinterpretation. "What we've found here is rare, and I'm unwilling to let it go without a fight."

Part of me wants to run from the intensity of his declaration. It's too much, too soon. We barely know each other. This could be nothing more than exceptional chemistry and the romance of a mountain getaway.

But another part—a part that's growing louder by the minute—recognizes the truth in his words. What I experienced with Cole in these brief encounters affects me more deeply than relationships that lasted months or even years.

"I need to think," I finally say, neither accepting nor rejecting his proposition. "This weekend has been... overwhelming, in the best possible way. But I need to process it."

He studies me, then nods, accepting my need for space without taking offense. "Fair enough." His hand finds mine again, squeezing gently. "Just promise me one thing."

"What's that?"

"Don't overthink it." His smile softens the command into a request. "Trust your instincts. They led you back here once already."

Before I can respond, my phone buzzes with a text. It's from the hospital: *ETA? Patients stable. OR team standing by.*

Reality intrudes with jarring finality. I show Cole the message with an apologetic grimace.

"I'll walk you to your car." Cole signals for the check.

The remaining breakfast and too-brief coffee are abandoned as we head back up to my room for my overnight bag, then down to the parking lot where my car waits. The morning is crisp and clear, and the mountain air is sharp with pine and possibility.

At my car, Cole takes my bag from my shoulder and places it in the back seat with the same casual authority he's displayed in every interaction. When he turns back to me, his expression is a complex blend of disappointment and understanding.

"Drive safely," he says, one hand coming up to cup my cheek. "Text me when you arrive, so I know you made it."

"I will," I promise, leaning into his touch.

"And Tess?" His thumb traces my lower lip, a gesture that's already become achingly familiar. "When you've had time to think, when you've processed everything that happened between us—call me. Whatever you decide, I want to hear it from you."

I nod, unable to find adequate words for the swirl of emotions his simple request evokes. Instead, I rise on tiptoes, pressing my lips to his in a kiss that starts gentle but quickly deepens as his arms wrap around me, pulling me firmly against him.

When we finally part, both slightly breathless, I see the same desire coursing through me reflected in his eyes. If I don't leave now, I might not leave at all.

"I have to go," I whisper against his lips.

"I know." He steps back, creating physical distance that does nothing to diminish the connection humming between us. "Go save lives, Dr. Carrington. It's what you do best."

He's partially wrong about that.

Yes, I save lives. I've trained for it. Built a whole identity around it.

But after this weekend... something shifted.

Because the thing I did *best*—the thing I felt most *alive* doing—was surrendering to him.

Obeying.

Yielding.

Letting go of control and finding something deeper in the freefall.

I haven't fully processed what that means, but it wasn't

just sex. It wasn't a fantasy. It was truth—unfiltered and undeniable.

And I want more of it. More of him.

The only problem?

I have no idea how this works in the real world. How do I balance the woman I've always been with the one he pulled out of me?

I need to figure that out. Because now that I've felt what it's like to be his... I don't want to be anything else.

The drive back to Denver is a blur of mountain switchbacks and racing thoughts. I replay every moment with Cole, from our snowed-in night at the clinic to our passionate reunion, searching for perspective, for clarity about what this connection means and what I want it to become.

By the time I reach the hospital, I've come no closer to answers. All I know is that something significant happened between us, which defies the neat categories and controlled parameters I usually apply to my life.

I park in the physicians' lot and check my appearance in the rearview mirror. Despite the early hour and hasty departure, I look surprisingly good—cheeks flushed with more than just mountain air, eyes bright with lingering excitement. If I didn't know better, I'd say I was glowing.

As promised, I text Cole before heading inside: *Arrived safely. Heading into surgery now. Will call when I can.*

His response comes immediately: *They're lucky to have you. So am I.*

The simple confidence in those last three words stays with me as I change into scrubs, as I review the patients' files, as I scrub in for the first complex vascular repair. It steadies my hands and focuses my mind, not as a distraction but as a reminder of the connection between competence and passion, between professional excellence and personal fulfillment.

Six hours later, I emerge from the second successful

surgery, exhausted but exhilarated. Both patients are stable, their complex vascular injuries repaired with techniques few surgeons in the region could have managed. It's the kind of work that reminds me why I chose this specialty and why I dedicated my life to the demanding, precise art of trauma surgery.

In the attending physicians' lounge, I collapse onto a couch, allowing myself a moment of professional satisfaction before the post-surgical documentation begins. My phone shows three missed calls from the hospital board and a text from Cole: *Thinking of you. Hope it went well.*

I smile at his message, typing a quick response: *Both surgeries successful. Exhausted but satisfied.*

Then I check my voicemail, listening as the board chair informs me that the CEO signed off on my appointment as department head, effective immediately. The position is mine, along with all the responsibility, prestige, and demands that come with it.

It should be a moment of pure triumph. This is what I've worked toward for years—the recognition of my skills, and the opportunity to shape trauma care at one of the region's premier hospitals. Yet, as I sit there, phone in hand, a curious ambivalence threads through my excitement.

I think of Cole's words at breakfast: *Denver is three hours away in good weather, four in bad. We both have demanding jobs with unpredictable schedules.* The new position will make my schedule more challenging and my availability more limited.

Can any relationship survive such constraints, especially one as new and untested as ours?

An email from the board chair interrupts my thoughts: *There will be a celebration dinner tomorrow night at Mazzio's at 7 PM. Bring a plus-one if you like. The board wants to officially welcome you.*

I stare at the message, finger hovering over the reply button. It's a plus-one—the perfect opportunity to integrate Cole into my professional world and merge our separate lives. But is that what I want?

Is that what *he* wants?

I'm still deliberating when my phone rings—this time, it's Cole himself. For a moment, I consider letting it go to voicemail. I'm exhausted and emotionally drained, and I'm not sure what to say about us or the future.

But something compels me to answer.

"Hello?"

"Hey." His voice, warm and deep, sends an immediate wave of comfort through me. "Bad time?"

"No, it's fine. I just finished the surgeries."

"Both successful, you said. That's incredible." The genuine admiration in his tone warms me more than any generic congratulations could. "How are you feeling?"

"Tired. Satisfied." I hesitate, then add, "And I just got word that I officially have the department head position."

"Congratulations!" His enthusiasm sounds completely sincere. "That's fantastic news. I know how much it means to you."

"Thank you." I close my eyes, leaning back against the couch. "They're having a celebration dinner tomorrow night," I find myself saying. "For the promotion. I'm allowed to bring someone."

"Are you asking me to come to Denver?" I can almost hear him considering this and weighing the implications.

"Would you want to?"

"Tess." My name in his mouth still sends a shiver through me. "I'd drive to Denver right now if you asked me to. But this isn't about what I want. It's about what you want, what you're ready for."

His willingness to put my needs first and give me space

while still making his interest clear resolves something in me. This man, whom I've known for a short time but who has deeply affected me, deserves honesty.

"I want to see where this goes," I tell him, the words coming easier than expected. "I don't know how we'll manage the distance or our schedules, but I want to try. If you do."

His relieved exhale is audible through the phone. "I do. More than I can express right now."

"So you'll come? Tomorrow? To the dinner?"

"Try to stop me." The smile in his voice is evident. "Text me the details, and I'll be there."

"Yes, sir." As I hang up, a curious peace settles over me. I've decided not just about tomorrow's dinner but about giving this unexpected connection a chance to grow into something more. The practical challenges remain, but the certainty that I'll see Cole again is enough to carry me through my exhaustion and doubts.

I gather my things, preparing to head home for a much-needed shower and rest before tomorrow's celebration. As I walk through the hospital corridors, nodding to colleagues and staff, I feel like I'm moving between worlds—the familiar professional realm I've inhabited for years and the new, unexplored territory that opened when a snowstorm forced me to seek shelter in a small mountain clinic.

What will happen when those worlds collide? When my colleagues meet the man who has so quickly and completely disrupted my carefully ordered life? When Cole sees me in my professional element, surrounded by the career ambitions that might challenge whatever is growing between us?

Angel's Peak

CHAPTER 8

———

REALITY CHECK

MAZZIO'S IS DENVER'S PREMIER ITALIAN restaurant, all dark wood panels and crisp white tablecloths, with a wine list that rivals any in the city. It's where hospital board members bring donors, where department heads celebrate major grants, and where medical royalty comes to see and be seen.

Tonight, I'm the guest of honor and a nervous wreck.

Not about the promotion—I've earned that through years of dedicated work and exceptional skill. No, my anxiety centers entirely on the man who will be arriving any minute to join me in this celebration.

I smooth the fabric of my midnight blue cocktail dress for the tenth time, checking my reflection in the restaurant's bathroom mirror. The dress is elegant but not overly formal, complementing my dark hair and complexion. It is professional enough for a work event but with a hint of allure in the way it skims my curves.

Will Cole like it? Will he be comfortable in this rarified atmosphere, so different from the rustic warmth of Angel's Peak? Will my colleagues see what I see in him, or will they dismiss him as just another rural healthcare provider, lacking the sophistication and ambition that drives our urban medical center?

The questions swirl in my mind as I apply a fresh coat of lipstick and take a steadying breath. This is ridiculous. I'm acting like a teenager before prom, not a newly appointed department head about to introduce a... what? Boyfriend seems too juvenile, and partner feels too presumptuous for our brief connection.

Whatever the label, Cole Blake has become important enough that I want him here tonight, important enough that his opinion of me—of this part of my life—matters more than perhaps it should.

When I return to the private dining room, several board members and key members of my department have already arrived. Dr. Samuel—my primary competition for the position—is noticeably absent, but that's no surprise. He's probably licking his wounds at the bar across town where surgical fellows gather to gossip and gripe.

"Dr. Carrington!" Dr. Eleanor Weiss, the board chairwoman, approaches with two glasses of champagne. "Here's our woman of the hour. You look lovely, my dear."

I accept the glass with a smile. "Thank you for organizing this, Eleanor. It means a lot to have the board's support."

"Well-deserved support," she corrects, clinking her glass against mine. "Your work on the Miller case alone would have secured this position. The rest is just icing on an already impressive cake."

We chat about the department's future direction, funding priorities, and research opportunities. It's comfortable territory, the kind of conversation I've been preparing for throughout my career. Yet part of me remains distracted, my gaze drifting repeatedly to the door.

Then suddenly, there he is.

Cole stands in the doorway, scanning the room with those intent blue eyes. He's wearing a charcoal gray suit that fits his broad shoulders perfectly. The effect is polished but not overly formal, a perfect balance of respect for the occasion without pretension.

When his gaze finds mine, everything else recedes—the murmur of conversation, the clink of glasses, Eleanor's voice still outlining some administrative priority. All I see is him.

All I feel is that same electric connection that sparked when I walked into his clinic a week ago.

"Excuse me," I murmur to Eleanor, not waiting for her response as I move toward the door.

Cole meets me halfway, a smile warming his features as he takes in my appearance. "You look beautiful," he says, voice pitched just for me despite the crowded room.

"You clean up pretty well yourself," I reply, trying for lightness despite the flutter in my stomach. "I wasn't sure you owned a suit up in Angel's Peak."

"Special occasions only." His hand finds the small of my back, warm and steady through the thin fabric of my dress. "Like celebrating my girlfriend's well-deserved promotion."

The casual label—girlfriend—should annoy me. I'm thirty-two years old, a respected surgeon, not some college student defining relationships on social media. Yet coming from him, with that quiet confidence, it feels right. A clear statement of intent and connection.

"Well, your girlfriend appreciates you driving all this way." I accept the designation with a smile. "How was the trip?"

"Uneventful, thankfully. Roads were clear." His gaze travels over the assembled group, assessing in the same efficient way I've seen him evaluate patients. "Quite the turnout."

"The hospital board rarely needs an excuse for an open bar." I joke, but there's an undercurrent of nervousness I can't quite hide. "Are you ready to meet them? I should warn you, they can be a bit..."

"Intimidating?" he supplies with a raised eyebrow. "Don't worry about me; I once talked down a grizzly bear that wandered into Mrs. Peterson's backyard while delivering her twins. I can handle a few hospital administrators."

The absurd claim startles a laugh out of me. "You did not."

"Well, it was a tiny bear. Possibly a large raccoon." His eyes crinkle with humor. "The point stands. I'm here for you, not to impress your colleagues."

The simple declaration settles something in me. Cole isn't intimidated by these people or this environment because he knows exactly who he is and what he brings to the table. It's the same quiet confidence that drew me to him from the start.

"Come on," I say, taking his hand. "There are some people I'd like you to meet."

The next hour passes in a blur of introductions and conversations. Cole charms Eleanor with his knowledge of her research on rural healthcare disparities, impresses the chief of surgery with pointed questions about our trauma protocols, and finds common ground with my colleagues through shared medical experiences. He's neither deferential nor arrogant, simply comfortable in his skin in a way that commands respect.

I watch him with growing admiration and, if I'm honest, a touch of surprise. I hadn't expected him to navigate these waters so skillfully, to hold his own among people who typically measure worth by institutional affiliations and publication records.

"Your date is quite something," Dr. Chen, one of my closest colleagues, murmurs as we stand by the appetizer table. "Not what I expected when you said you were bringing someone from that mountain clinic."

"What did you expect?" I ask, curious about how others see him.

She shrugs, sipping her wine. "I don't know. Someone more... provincial, I guess? He's very well-informed, very articulate." She gives me a sidelong glance. "And incredibly hot, which I'm sure hasn't escaped your notice."

"It may have come to my attention, yes." I rush of heat rises in my cheeks.

"So this is serious? You and the mountain doctor?"

The question catches me off guard. Is it serious?

We've barely known each other, yet we spent two incredible nights together. Three if you count the night of the storm. By any reasonable standard, this is nothing more than the beginning of a *potential* relationship, too new and untested to be called serious.

Yet when I look across the room to where Cole is deep in conversation with the chief of surgery, something in my chest tightens with a certainty that defies such rational assessment.

"It's... evolving," I tell Chen, which is both true and entirely inadequate.

She follows my gaze, her expression softening. "Well, for what it's worth, he hasn't taken his eyes off you all night. Even when fully engaged in conversation. He tracks your movements like you're the most important person in the room."

I hadn't noticed, but now that she mentions it, Cole has positioned himself throughout the evening to keep me in his line of sight. It's not possessive or controlling, just... attentive. As if maintaining our connection across the crowded room is as natural and necessary as breathing.

The realization warms me, adding to the glow of the evening's success. My colleagues respect me, the board supports my vision for the department, and I have this remarkable man by my side, watching over me even as he establishes his presence among my professional peers.

After dinner, Dr. Weiss offers a toast, praising my surgical skills and leadership potential with genuine enthusiasm. I respond with appropriate gratitude and a brief outline of my goals for the trauma department, earning approving nods from the assembled group.

As the formal part of the evening concludes and people mingle again, Cole appears at my side, hand settling lightly on my lower back. The simple touch, now familiar, grounds me amid the swirl of professional congratulations.

"Proud of you," he murmurs close to my ear. "You're going to be an exceptional department head."

Something in his tone makes me look up sharply. "But?"

His smile is gentle but tinged with something I can't quite identify. "No 'but.' Just pride. You've worked hard for this. You deserve it."

I study his face, sensing an undercurrent he's not expressing. "Let's get some air," I suggest, nodding toward the restaurant's small terrace. "It's getting warm in here."

The night is cool but not uncomfortable; the terrace is empty except for us. City lights stretch below, so different from the star-filled mountain skies of Angel's Peak. Cole leans against the railing, loosening his collar with one finger as he gazes at the urban landscape.

"Beautiful view," he comments. "Different from home, but beautiful in its own way."

"Cole." I move to stand beside him, close enough that our shoulders touch. "What's on your mind? And don't say 'nothing'—I've seen that look before."

He turns to face me, those blue eyes serious now. "I was just thinking about what this means for us."

"What?"

"This." He gestures toward the dining room behind us. "Your promotion. The responsibilities that come with it." His hand finds mine on the railing, fingers intertwining with quiet certainty. "You're about to take on a major leadership role at one of the top hospitals in the region. That means longer hours, more administrative headaches, politics, pressure, and very little room for anything else—especially something like this."

He says it gently, but it lands hard.

"I know that." The defensive edge in my voice is sharp. "I've worked toward this for years. I know exactly what it entails."

"I'm not questioning that." His voice doesn't rise. Doesn't match my heat. It stays steady. Grounded. Unshakable. "I know you earned this. You deserve every piece of it." He looks at me like he means it. Like he's proud. "But it complicates things between us. And pretending otherwise doesn't change the reality."

The truth of his words slices through the fog of accomplishment and adrenaline.

He's right.

The title I just accepted comes with a cost. And I've always been willing to pay it.

Until now.

"So what are you saying?" I ask, even though I know. Even though I dread the answer. "That we should end this before it even begins?"

"No."

The word is immediate. Unyielding.

"I'm saying we need to be honest about what we're up against. The distance. The time. The way our lives demand everything from us." He shifts, facing me fully. His fingers tighten around mine. "But if we both want it badly enough, we can make it work. The question is—do you *want* it? Do you want me enough to fight for this when it's inconvenient and hard and messy?"

Cole's gaze pins me. It's not an accusation—it's an invitation.

But it still scares the hell out of me.

"I do." My voice is quiet. Honest. "I want it, but I'm scared." The words rip from somewhere deep—past the pride, past the practiced calm. "I've given everything to this career. Sacrificed friendships, family, sleep, everything to be the best." I look away. My throat tightens. "And now I'm standing here thinking—what if I can't be the best at both? What if loving you means I fail somewhere else? Or worse... what if I fail you?"

The admission leaves me bare.

He doesn't flinch.

"Then we fail together," he says. Just like that. No hesitation. No doubt. "And we get back up together. But I'd rather try and fall flat than let you walk away pretending this didn't mean something."

I exhale shakily, my heart thudding like it's trying to climb into his hand.

"Just like you," I whisper, echoing his words from that night by the fire, "I don't do things halfway. Not in my work. Not in my life."

"I've noticed," he murmurs, a hint of a smile playing at the edge of his mouth. "It's one of many things I admire about you."

But something inside me trembles loose. Something I've kept hidden beneath years of control and focus.

"I don't know how to do this," I admit, barely breathing. "I've never made space for someone like you. It terrifies me."

His expression shifts—something fierce behind the softness.

He steps closer, one hand rising to cradle the side of my face. His thumb brushes over my cheek, grounding me.

"Then let me say it for both of us," he murmurs. "I've fallen for you."

My breath stutters.

"I knew it the second you walked into that clinic. Love at first sight." His voice is steady, unapologetic. "It hit me like a freight train, and I haven't stopped thinking about you since." He leans in, forehead pressing lightly to mine, anchoring me with nothing more than presence. "I'm not scared of this. Not even a little. Because what we have?" His gaze doesn't waver. "It's real. It's rare."

Then his voice drops—low, resolute. Certain.

"And it's worth every mile, every sacrifice, every fight it takes to keep. Now, all I need you to do is believe that you can have both. Your ambition... and something real with me."

He doesn't ask. He states.

Something in me responds to that—like muscle memory, like instinct.

I take a breath, gathering courage for the kind of honesty I don't often let myself voice.

"What I feel when I'm with you—it's different. Stronger. Deeper. More..." I struggle to name it. "More real somehow."

His hand tightens around mine—steady, grounding. "I feel it, too."

"But my career is real too," I continue, voice firmer. "This position, this hospital—it's not just my job. It's my purpose.

"I know," he says, voice even. "And I'd never ask you to give that up."

"Then what is it about? Because it feels like you're asking me to choose."

He shakes his head, frustration briefly crossing his features. "No. I'm asking you to consider making room for both. For your career and for us." His free hand cups my cheek, thumb tracing my jawline. "I'm asking if you believe what we have is worth the effort it will take to nurture it alongside your professional responsibilities."

When he puts it that way, the answer seems obvious. Of course, it's worth fighting for. The connection between us, as new and unexpected as it is, has already affected me more deeply than relationships that lasted years.

"I do," I admit softly.

His expression softens, understanding replacing frustration. "We figure it out together. Day by day. We make plans when we can, use technology when we can't be physically together, and communicate honestly and directly about what's working and what isn't."

The practical approach appeals to my logical nature. No grand promises or unrealistic expectations, just a commitment to try, to work at it, to value what we're building enough to weather the inevitable challenges.

"It won't be easy," I warn, echoing his earlier assessment.

"The best things rarely are." His thumb traces my lower lip, a gesture that's become achingly familiar in our brief time together. "But you're worth it, Dr. Carrington. The question is whether you think I am."

The vulnerability beneath his confident exterior touches me deeply. This strong, capable man who commands every room he enters is letting me see his uncertainty and his need for reassurance that I value this connection as much as he does.

Rather than answer with words, I rise on tiptoes to press my lips to his, pouring into the kiss everything I'm still learning to express. My belief in us, my commitment to trying, and my growing certainty that what we've found is too precious to sacrifice on the altar of career ambition or practical concerns.

When we part, slightly breathless, I find the words I need.

"You're worth it."

The smile that breaks across his face, warm and genuine, makes my heart flip in my chest. "Good," he says simply, pulling me closer. "Because I'm not giving up on you. Not without one hell of a fight."

The conviction in his voice steadies me, anchoring me against the swirl of doubts and fears. Cole Blake may have entered my life by accident, a random consequence of a mountain snowstorm, but keeping him there will be a deliberate choice—one I'm increasingly certain I want to make.

Our moment of connection is interrupted by the glass door sliding open, revealing Dr. Weiss with an apologetic smile.

"Sorry to intrude," she says, though her knowing look suggests she's not sorry at all. "The CEO just arrived and wants to congratulate you personally."

"I'll be right there," I promise, reluctantly stepping away from Cole's embrace.

When Eleanor retreats, Cole doesn't let me go.

His hand tightens at my waist, pulling me back into him until my spine meets the solid heat of his chest.

His mouth dips to my ear, and his voice is a slow, sinful growl.

"Go be brilliant."

The words are soft. Deceptively sweet.

But then—his teeth scrape my earlobe, and everything shifts.

"While they're raising glasses and telling you how impressive you are…" His palm flattens over my stomach, holding me in place. "I'll be thinking about how fast I can get you out of this dress. How fast I can get you on your knees."

My breath catches.

"I want to see that proud mouth open for me. I want to feel your lips stretch around my cock while you look up at me and obey."

His voice turns darker. Silk over steel.

"I brought toys tonight."

The words slam through me, straight to my core.

"Leather cuffs. Real ones. Bought them for you." His lips graze the edge of my jaw. "A velvet gag to keep you quiet when you're screaming into the mattress."

I whimper, and his smile curves against my skin.

"And a crop." The word lands like a strike. "So when you're tied down and begging to come, I can remind you exactly who you belong to."

Heat floods me. Arousal twists tight and fast, blooming everywhere at once.

His hand drifts lower, slow, possessive.

"I'm going to spread you out, cuff you to my bed, and make you wait. Make you feel every single second of what it means to be mine."

I bite back a moan.

He pulls back just enough to see my face, eyes blazing with hunger and power.

"Now go." His voice is low. Absolute. "Smile. Nod. Accept their praise like the good girl you are." He leans in, one last whisper pressed to the shell of my ear. "Because after this party ends... you'll serve me."

Back inside, the room swells with voices and laughter and light, but I'm already on fire.

My legs tremble beneath the weight of his promises. My skin burns where he touched me. My lips ache to say *Yes, Sir* even in a room full of my peers.

Every glass of champagne is laced with the taste of anticipation. Every handshake feels distant.

Because I'm not thinking about my title. Or the applause.

I'm thinking about cuffs.

A gag.

A crop.

His control.

And the moment he finally makes good on every filthy promise.

I watch him move through the crowd, at ease among these medical elites, and feel a surge of something that might be pride, possessiveness, or the beginning of something deeper than I'm ready to name. His confidence is quiet but undeniable.

He speaks with the hospital board chair like he belongs here—because he does.

What he said to me stays with me throughout the evening, a warm current beneath the professional satisfaction of this career milestone. No one in this room knows what I know.

They see calm, composed Dr. Carrington accepting accolades and shaking hands.

They don't see the ache beneath my smile.

The heat curling low and steady between my thighs.

The countdown running in my head.

If they had any idea what I'd be doing later tonight.

Not leading a prestigious department. Not delivering another keynote or drafting policy.

But kneeling.

Obedient and ready.

Waiting for a man who's completely, unapologetically rewritten the rules of who I thought I had to be.

My knees pressed into soft carpet. My wrists bound in cuffs he bought just for me. A gag at the ready in case I get too loud when he denies me just to hear me beg.

They'd never believe it.

And maybe that's what makes it even more intoxicating.

The secret. The surrender. The thrill of giving up every ounce of control in private... after spending my life projecting nothing but power in public.

I glance at Cole. He's mid-conversation, but he must feel it

—because his gaze cuts to mine through the crowd like a blade.

Heat. Hunger. Command.

And just like that, I'm burning again.

I want this night to end. Need it to.

Because no award, title, or standing ovation can compare to what's waiting for me when this is over.

Later, we'll figure out the practical details of distance and schedules, of professional obligations and personal needs. We'll map the terrain of this unexpected connection, defining boundaries and expectations with the same care we'd approach a complex procedure.

For now, it's enough to feel his steady presence beside me as I accept congratulations on my professional achievement, knowing that when the public celebration ends, a more private one awaits.

But after this night ends?

I want to fall to my knees and thank him for ruining me. For showing me who I can be when I let go.

The second these champagne glasses empty, the second the last handshake ends—

This isn't the future I envisioned when I drove to Angel's Peak a week ago, seeking nothing more than a brief escape from my demanding career. As I glance at Cole, catching the warmth in his eyes as he discusses trauma protocols with the chief of surgery, I realize I'm already his.

Sometimes, the detours are more valuable than the destination. And sometimes, getting caught in that snowstorm was the luckiest wrong turn I could've taken.

Angel's Peak

Chapter 9

Heart vs. Head

My apartment looks different with Cole in it.

This thought strikes me as we step through the door, the celebration dinner behind us. The sleek, modern space I've carefully curated—all clean lines and neutral tones, more showcase than sanctuary—suddenly seems sterile, impersonal compared to the vibrant energy he brings into it.

He moves through my living room with the same quiet confidence he displays everywhere, taking in the minimalist furnishings, the abstract art, and the conspicuous absence of personal touches.

"Very you," he comments, running a finger along the edge of my glass coffee table.

"What does that mean?" I ask, setting my purse down and slipping off my heels.

He turns, that perceptive gaze taking me in from head to toe. "Elegant. Accomplished. Carefully controlled." His mouth quirks in a half-smile. "Beautiful but a little untouchable."

The assessment is uncomfortably accurate. My home, like

my life, has been designed to impress rather than invite, to project success rather than reveal vulnerability.

"Would you like a drink?" I offer, needing a moment to regain my equilibrium. "I have wine, whiskey, or I could make coffee."

"Water is fine." He shrugs off his suit jacket and drapes it neatly over a chair. The simple action—making himself at home in my space—sends a curious flutter through my stomach. "It's been a long day."

In the kitchen, I fill two glasses from the filtered dispenser in my refrigerator, using the mundane task to center myself. When I return to the living room, Cole has moved to the floor-to-ceiling windows that showcase the city lights thirty floors below.

"Quite a view," he says, accepting the water without looking away from the urban panorama. "Different from mine."

"Better or worse?" I ask, genuinely curious about how he sees my world.

He considers this, sipping his water before answering. "Neither. Just different." His free hand finds mine, fingers intertwining with casual intimacy. "Yours shows humanity's accomplishments. Mine shows nature's. Both have their merits."

The diplomatic response makes me smile. "Very politically correct, Dr. Blake."

His laugh is low and warm. "Fine. I prefer my mountain sunrises to your city lights, but I can appreciate the view nonetheless." His gaze shifts from the window to my face, intensity replacing humor. "Especially when it includes you in that dress."

The heat in his eyes sends a spark of electricity down my spine. We've been dancing around this moment all evening—maintaining professional decorum at the dinner while the memory of our previous intimacy hummed between us like a current.

"You've been very patient tonight," I observe, setting my water down on a side table. "Very... proper."

"Professional," he corrects, his voice dropping to that register that resonates directly in my core. "There's a time and place for everything, Dr. Carrington. Your colleagues didn't need to see how badly I've wanted to touch you all night."

The blunt admission pulls a soft gasp from me. This is what continues to disarm me about Cole—his absolute directness and his refusal to play the games of hint and suggestion that characterize most early relationships.

"And now?" I ask, emboldened by his candor.

He sets his glass down. "Now we're alone, and there's nothing stopping me from showing you exactly what I've been thinking about since I saw you in that dress." His eyes hold mine, gauging my reaction. "Unless you'd rather keep talking."

"No, sir." The choice is clear, and my body has already decided even as my mind catches up. "I think we've talked enough for tonight."

His smile is slow and predatory. "Good."

In two steps, he closes the distance between us, one hand sliding into my hair at the nape of my neck, the other circling my waist to pull me firmly against him. Like our previous encounters, there's no hesitation, no careful testing of boundaries. He claims my mouth with absolute certainty, his kiss deep and demanding from the first contact.

I yield immediately, opening to him as my arms wind around his neck. His taste—now familiar but no less intoxicating—sends heat racing through my veins, pooling low in my belly. His hand tightens in my hair, angling my head to deepen the kiss further, his tongue exploring my mouth with a thoroughness that leaves me breathless.

When we finally break apart, his eyes darken to midnight

blue as his pupils dilate with desire. His breathing is slightly ragged, matching my own.

"Bedroom." The single word is somehow both a question and a command.

I nod, not trusting my voice, and take his hand to lead him down the hallway. My bedroom continues the apartment's modern aesthetic—a platform bed with crisp white linens, minimalist furniture, and another wall of windows offering the same spectacular view.

Cole takes it in with a glance before his attention returns to me. He moves with deliberate purpose, hands coming up to frame my face as he kisses me again, softer this time but no less intent.

"Turn around," he murmurs against my lips.

I comply, shivering with anticipation as his fingers find the zipper at the back of my dress. He lowers it with tantalizing slowness, his knuckles brushing my spine in a deliberate caress that makes my skin tingle. When the zipper reaches its end, just above the small of my back, his hands slide beneath the loosened fabric to my shoulders, easing the dress down my arms until it pools at my feet in a puddle of silken fabric.

I stand before him in nothing but a strapless black bra and matching lace panties, feeling strangely vulnerable despite our previous intimacy. There's something different about this encounter—something more deliberate, more meaningful than our passionate reunion at the lodge.

His sharp intake of breath is deeply satisfying, as is the barely restrained hunger in his eyes as they travel over my body.

"Christ, Tess," he breathes, his voice rough with desire. "You're perfect."

Before I can respond, he pulls me to him, his mouth finding mine in a kiss that's equal parts tenderness and possession. His hands explore the newly exposed skin of my back, my waist, and my hips, learning the curves and planes of my body with exquisite attention.

When we part, I reach for his shirt's buttons, wanting to feel his skin against mine. He captures my wrists in one large hand.

"Remember what I told you before? About how I lead?" His voice is gentle but firm with the reminder.

My pulse quickens. "I remember."

"Good." He releases my wrists, bringing one hand up to trace my lower lip with his thumb. "I plan on taking my time tonight. I want to find every spot that makes you gasp, every touch that makes you tremble." His eyes hold mine, ensuring I understand. "You'll learn how to beg and suffer for me. Please me."

He steps back, creating a small space between us.

"On the bed." His tone makes it clear this is not a suggestion.

I move to comply, sitting on the edge of my four-poster bed, suddenly very aware of my near-nakedness compared to his still-clothed state. Rather than join me immediately, he unbuttons his shirt with deliberate slowness, never taking his eyes from mine.

The gradual reveal of his torso—broad shoulders, muscled chest dusted with dark hair, flat stomach with a trail disappearing into his slacks—is a performance designed to build anticipation. It's devastatingly effective. By the time he shrugs the shirt from his shoulders, my breathing has quickened, and my skin flushes with desire.

"Like what you see?" The question teases, but his eyes are serious, wanting genuine confirmation.

"Yes, sir," I admit, allowing myself to appreciate his body openly. "Very much."

"Good. Because I can't get enough of looking at you." His smile is satisfied but not smug.

He steps forward, positioning himself between my knees, one hand coming up to cup my cheek. The tender gesture amid the heated moment tightens my chest with an emotion I'm not ready to name.

"I'm going to touch you now," he says, his voice dropping lower. "Everywhere. And I want to hear every sound. I want to know exactly what you like, what drives you crazy, what makes you come apart in my hands. No holding back. Understand?"

The explicit instruction, delivered in that commanding tone, sends heat flooding through me.

"I understand."

"Good." He leans down to claim my mouth again, the kiss deep and thorough, before trailing his lips along my jawline to the sensitive spot just below my ear. When he finds it, I gasp, my head falling back to give him better access.

"There," he murmurs approvingly. "Like that."

His mouth continues its exploration, tracking down my throat to my collarbone while his hands move to my back, deftly unhooking my bra. When the garment falls away, he draws back slightly to take in the newly revealed skin, eyes darkening with appreciation.

"Perfect," he says again, cupping the weight of one breast in his palm, thumb brushing over the nipple in a light caress that makes me arch toward him.

"Cole," I breathe, already aching for more.

"Patience," he admonishes gently, even as his touch grows more purposeful, rolling the hardened peak between thumb and forefinger. "We have all night."

His mouth replaces his hand, hot and wet around my nipple, while his fingers attend to its twin. The dual sensation pulls a moan from deep in my throat, my hands tangling in his hair.

He works me this way for long minutes, alternating between breasts, using lips and tongue, the occasional scrape of teeth in a symphony of sensation that has me writhing beneath his touch. Just when I think I can't bear any more without some relief where I need it most, he moves lower—trailing kisses down my sternum, across my ribs, to the sensitive skin of my stomach.

His hands find my hips, fingers hooking into the waistband of my panties. He pauses—then looks up.

That look alone sends a shiver through me.

He drags the lace down my legs with torturous slowness. His gaze locked on mine as he removes the final barrier between us.

Now fully naked, I fight the urge to cover myself. Instead, I hold his gaze—and that's when he reaches for something behind him on the bed.

My breath catches.

Leather.

Angel's Peak

CHAPTER 10

NO MERCY

THICK BLACK LEATHER CUFFS. SOFT INSIDE, SLEEK and firm on the outside, with polished metal buckles and a locking clasp. His fingers stroke one as he lifts it, like he's handling something precious. His voice is quiet but rough with intent.

"I had these made for you." He shows me the lining—buttery-soft against skin. Then rotates them slowly, letting me see the contrast—the soft restraint inside, the undeniable authority on the outside. "They'll hold you without bruising." His gaze lifts. "But make no mistake. Once they're on, you won't be moving."

My pulse jumps.

He takes my wrist gently, reverently, fitting the first cuff and buckling it tight. Not harsh—but final. The quiet click of the lock sounds louder than thunder in the space between us.

The second cuff follows, and he guides my arms slowly, deliberately, up over my head.

"Do you trust me?"

The question is soft, but it lands like a command.

"Yes," I whisper, breath shaking.

He stills. Just for a moment. Then his gaze lifts to mine—calm, unflinching.

"I told you what I expect when we're like this." His voice doesn't rise. It doesn't need to. It wraps around me like silk drawn tight.

I swallow, pulse hammering.

"Yes, Sir."

"Good girl." A flicker of satisfaction passes through his expression.

He threads the attached straps around the bedposts—anchoring me. Spreading me.

Open. Exposed. Offered.

Before he steps back, he leans in, mouth close to my ear. "One more thing," he murmurs, tone quieter now—reverent. "You can stop this at any time. If anything feels wrong, too much, not right, you say the word." He brushes his knuckles down my cheek. "Your safe word is Mercy."

The word lands like a tether.

Security.

Control without cruelty. Power, but never without care.

"Say it once for me."

"Mercy." I meet his eyes.

He nods, brushing his thumb over my lip with a look that says he heard me and he'll never forget it. Then he stands and begins to undress—his eyes never leaving mine. When the last piece falls, he stands before me, naked, hard, and devastating. I feel it in every part of me.

Not just arousal.

Devotion.

His mouth hovers just above me, breath warm against slick, sensitive skin.

"You were so good for me back at the lodge," he murmurs, his voice thick, ragged. "So responsive. So fucking sweet when you came all over my mouth."

I gasp, hips jerking.

"But tonight?" His gaze lifts—dark, ravenous. "Tonight's different." His hand slides up my thigh, slow, purposeful. A tease and a threat all at once. "Tonight's not about what you want, sweetheart." He kisses the inside of my knee, then another higher. "Tonight... is about me."

My breath catches.

"What I want." Another kiss, dangerously close. "What I take." His fingers curl around my thighs, spreading me wider, locking me open to him. "And right now, I want to taste you until you can't fucking breathe."

Then—he does.

No preamble. No hesitation.

Just his mouth. Hot. Greedy. Unrelenting.

I cry out, the sound ragged and raw. My hips buck, but his hands clamp down, holding me in place, giving me no escape.

"You're mine like this," he growls between strokes, tongue fucking me with ruthless precision. "Tied down, spread open, dripping for me."

His fingers dig into my thighs, controlling every twitch, every attempt to move.

"You can't stop me," he says, lips dragging over my clit, tongue circling mercilessly. "You're not *allowed* to stop me. You gave me control, remember?"

My fingers fist the sheets. I can't speak, can barely breathe.

"That means I get to make you come as many times as I want." A lick, slow and devastating. "Keep you on the edge for hours if I feel like it."

"Cole..." I sob his name.

"Beg me for it. Let me hear how much you need my mouth. My fingers. My cock." His voice is filth and command wrapped in velvet. "Beg me like the good girl you are."

I'm too far gone for shame.

"Please—please let me come. I'm so close, I need it—need you."

His groan is savage, primal.

"You fucking will, sweetheart. Again and again."

And then—two fingers slide inside me, curling just right, stroking that place that makes my vision blur. His tongue flicks faster, relentless against my clit. The sounds echoing in the room—wet, obscene, desperate—are mine.

I shatter.

Screaming. Thrashing. Held down and claimed.

But he doesn't stop.

Doesn't even slow.

"That's one," he growls. "Now, let's see how many more I can wring out of you before you pass out."

He slides two fingers inside me while his mouth returns to its exquisite torture. The combination of internal and external stimulation quickly builds toward an orgasm that promises to be even more intense than before.

"Let me hear you," he commands against my sensitive flesh. "Don't hold back. Let go for me."

The permission—or perhaps the command—breaks the last of my control. I come with his name on my lips, body arching off the bed as pleasure crashes through me in waves. He works me through it, gentling his touch but not stopping until the last tremor subsides and I collapse boneless against the sheets.

I'm still shaking.

Every nerve lit up, every muscle twitching with aftershocks.

But he doesn't give me time to recover. Doesn't even pause to let me catch my breath.

Instead, the mattress shifts. The heat of his body rising, climbing over me.

Claiming me.

His hands brace beside my head, arms caging me in, and when I force my eyes open, he's there—hovering above me, jaw tight, eyes black with hunger. Still fully in control. Still hard.

And fuck—he's gorgeous like this.

Hair messy, mouth wet with me, body radiating heat and power and intent. His cock presses against my thigh, hot and heavy and insistent.

"Look at you," he murmurs, voice wrecked and reverent. "Fucking destroyed. And I haven't even been inside you yet."

A whimper escapes me.

"I'm not done with you." He leans in, nose brushing mine, his breath a warning. "I'm not even close." His tone turns darker—rough silk wrapped around steel.

His mouth finds my throat, teeth scraping the sensitive skin.

"You think two orgasms are enough for me?" His voice is a low, dangerous promise. "I want to feel you come again. And again. Until you can't think. Until you forget your name, your title, every fucking thing except how good I make you feel." He pulls back just enough to meet my eyes. "I'm going to fuck you so deep, you'll feel me in the morning."

A broken sound leaves my lips—half breath, half need.

"Is that what you want, sweetheart?" he whispers, mouth brushing mine, teasing. "You want me to use you? To keep you tied down?"

I nod frantically. "Yes—please. God, yes, sir, *please*."

His smile is slow. Dangerous. Triumphant.

"That's my girl."

Then he reaches between us, guiding his cock to my entrance—teasing, just barely there.

"You're going to take every inch," he murmurs, dragging it through my slick folds. "Because that's what you do for me, isn't it?"

"Yes, Sir."

He doesn't ease in.

He thrusts deep on the first stroke—all of him—stretching me wide, filling me to the hilt in a single, devastating push.

I cry out, the sound raw and feral, echoing off the walls.

He doesn't stop. Doesn't give me time to adjust. Because this isn't about tenderness. It's for him, and it's about *claiming*.

His hips slam into mine, fast and punishing, the slap of skin on skin obscene and perfect. My wrists strain against the cuffs with every thrust, body arching to meet him, to take more.

"Fuck—yes," he grits, voice jagged. "You feel that?"

"Oh my god—"

"You were made for this. For me." He drives in harder. Deeper. The headboard creaks in rhythm with his pace. "This tight little pussy was built to take my cock."

My breath shatters. My body burns.

He leans down, grabbing my throat—not squeezing, just holding. Owning.

"Say it," he growls. "Say you're mine."

"I'm yours," I gasp. "Yours."

"Fucking right you are." He releases my neck only to slam into me harder, the bed jolting beneath us. His other hand grips my thigh, hiking it higher, giving him even deeper access.

I feel every inch of him. Every brutal, perfect thrust. Every filthy word that falls from his mouth is a brand on my skin.

"You love this," he snarls, watching my face as he pounds into me. "Being used. Being wrecked. Being mine."

"Oh my god—yes—"

"You're going to come for me again." His thumb slides down to circle my clit. Fast. Relentless. No mercy. "And you're going to scream when you do."

I'm already there.

The orgasm rips through me without warning—violent, consuming, obliterating.

I scream, back bowing off the bed, body shaking against the restraints.

And still, he doesn't stop.

"Fuck, that's it—look at you." His voice is wrecked. Reverent. Ruthless. "Falling apart like you were fucking built for me." He fucks me through it, chasing his release.

With a guttural sound, he slams deep and stays there, hips grinding against mine as he pulses inside me, thick and hot, groaning my name like a curse and a prayer. He stays braced above me, arms trembling, jaw clenched.

And for a moment, the only sound is our breathing— harsh, ragged, sated.

He withdraws slowly, deliberately, letting the stretch and loss burn. I whimper, still shaking, wrecked in the best way. But even before I can fully collapse into the mattress, he's moving.

Not away.

Not to clean up.

But to continue.

He stands beside the bed, breathing heavy, chest slick with sweat. His cock—still wet from me—rests thick and half-hard against his thigh, but I can already see the stir of life returning to it. He's far from finished.

And then I see what he's holding.

More black leather.

A slim crop. Elegant. Dangerous. The tip just slightly curved. A weapon crafted for precision.

Angel's Peak

Chapter 11

The Edge of Pleasure

He lifts the crop slowly, deliberately, letting me watch. Letting me anticipate.

The tip taps once against his palm.

A sharp, clean sound—

And my breath catches.

Fear flickers. Not terror—no. But something primal. Instinctive. A spike of adrenaline that makes my pulse stutter and my skin prickle with awareness.

I've never done this. Never imagined I would.

Pain, used like this—meant for pleasure, not punishment—isn't something I've ever considered.

But Cole has.

"You did well," he says, voice still gravel and heat. "So good. So fucking tight when you came, but I'm not done with you, sweetheart. Not even close."

He walks to the foot of the bed, the crop gripped in his strong hand like an extension of his will, and I can't look away.

Can't breathe.

Can't stop the heat that pulses low in my belly—thick, liquid, undeniable.

"I want to teach you something new," he murmurs, tracing lazy lines over my ribs. "How pain—*the right kind*—can make the pleasure sweeter."

He drags the crop slowly across my stomach, teasing. Not striking. Not yet. Up between my breasts. Over the soft swell of flesh. Across the straps binding my wrists above my head.

"Tell me..." He leans in, voice low and lethal, the crop trailing lazy patterns over my ribs. "Do you want to feel it?" His mouth brushes my collarbone, heat bleeding into skin. "A taste of my crop?"

The crop lifts—taps lightly against my inner thigh. Another tap. Higher.

"Do you want me to make you burn?" His gaze finds mine, dark and patient. Waiting. Wanting. "Say it."

I shudder, breath catching. Words fail me and all I can do is nod.

The crop taps once—harder—against my thigh. A warning.

"Not like that. Not some wordless plea." His voice sharpens, silk over steel. "Use your words, sweetheart. Show me you're mine."

I swallow hard, pulse thundering in my ears. My thighs tremble, not from fear—but anticipation.

The line between threat and thrill blurs.

"Say it," he repeats, stepping closer, dragging the crop up my stomach in a slow, deliberate line. "Tell me you want to burn for me."

My voice wavers, but it doesn't break.

"I want to burn for you, Sir."

His smile is slow. Dark.

"Good girl."

The first strike lands on the inside of my thigh. A sharp, stinging kiss.

I gasp.

It's not unbearable. It's precise. And followed by the slow slide of his fingers over the same spot—stroking, soothing, claiming.

"That's it," he breathes. "Breathe through it. Take it for me."

Another. Higher.

The sting. The touch. The praise.

The world narrows to leather and heat, and his voice anchoring me through it all.

I'm floating.

"You're doing so good. So beautiful like this. Bound and exposed and letting me shape your pleasure."

Another strike. Another brush of his fingers.

My thighs tremble. My breath comes in pants.

And somewhere between pain and praise, I feel it—need rising again. Arousal twisting sharp and fast, rewiring my understanding of surrender all over again.

He climbs back onto the bed, and when he presses his body to mine—hot, hard, demanding—I feel his cock, thick and ready, sliding against my thigh. He thrusts in with a sound that's all possession and hunger, grinding into me with brutal purpose.

"I'm going to fuck you until your legs don't work."

And I can only moan, already unraveling all over again.

His forehead rests against mine as he gives me time to adjust to his size.

"Christ, you feel good," he murmurs, voice strained with the effort of remaining still. "So tight, so perfect."

When he moves, it's with the same deliberate control he displayed before—each thrust measured, angled to hit exactly the right spot within me. His eyes never leave mine, maintaining that connection that's become as important as the physical joining.

"Wrap your legs around me," he instructs, one hand sliding

beneath me to lift my hips slightly, changing the angle to drive even deeper.

I comply eagerly, ankles locking at the small of his back, allowing him even greater access. The new position sends him deeper, hitting a spot that makes me gasp with each thrust.

"That's it," he encourages, the pace increasing slightly. "Take all of me. You're doing so well, taking me so perfectly."

The praise, combined with the exquisite fullness of him inside me, quickly rebuilds the pleasure I thought momentarily spent. I move with him, meeting each thrust, feeling the controlled power in each movement.

"Cole," I gasp as the familiar tension begins to coil low in my belly. "I'm close—again."

"I know," he murmurs, never breaking rhythm. "I can feel you tightening around me. So responsive, so perfect for me." One hand slides between us, finding the sensitive bundle of nerves at my center. "Come for me again. Let me feel you come around my cock."

The explicit command, combined with the added stimulation, sends me over the edge. This orgasm is deeper, more intense than the first, radiating outward from where we're joined to consume my entire body. I cry out his name as the pleasure crests and breaks.

He follows me moments later, his rhythm faltering as his release claims him. His face in that moment of abandon is the most beautiful thing I've ever seen—the usual control giving way to raw, unfiltered pleasure, my name a rough prayer on his lips as he empties himself inside me.

Afterward, he collapses beside me rather than on top of me, immediately drawing me into his arms. We lie there in silence for several minutes, just breathing together as our heart rates gradually slow.

His hand traces idle patterns on my hip, his breathing steady against my hair. The simple intimacy of the moment—

this quiet aftermath—feels almost more significant than the passionate joining that preceded it.

Time loses meaning.

What begins as hunger turns into ritual—worship through control.

He uses me.

Again.

And again.

And again.

Between orgasms, he doesn't stop.

He teaches about pleasure, pain, discipline, and obedience.

The cuffs stay on all night—sometimes securing my wrists to the bedposts, sometimes behind my back, sometimes above my head as he flips me, bends me, repositions me like I belong to him.

Because I do.

The crop makes return visits—sharper on my ass, more delicate along the curve of my breasts, occasionally between my thighs when I whimper without permission. But always followed by his mouth. His praise. His touch.

He balances the sting with sweetness so expertly it feels like devotion.

When I get too loud, he introduces the gag. Black velvet. Soft but final. He slides it between my lips with reverence, buckles it behind my head with care, and watches me fall apart for him, wordless and wide-eyed.

"Look at you," he murmurs, stroking my cheek as I moan around the gag. "Bound. Gagged. So fucking perfect."

He makes me come while gagged. Then removes it only to demand, "Thank me properly."

And I do.

He lets me ride him until I can barely hold myself up, only to flip me and thrust from behind, one hand on my throat, the other pulling my cuffs like reins.

Each orgasm feels different. Sharper. Deeper. Like he's not just breaking me—but rewriting me.

He tells me I'm his. That I was made for this. That no one will ever fuck me like this again because no one will own me like this. By the time dawn edges across the sky in soft grays and golds, I'm limp and trembling, my body exhausted but my soul burning.

He finally unbuckles the cuffs and pulls me into his chest, one hand smoothing gently over my hair, the other wrapped protectively around my waist.

Not a word is spoken.

There's no need.

He knows.

I know.

I came to Angel's Peak in control.

And now I'm wrapped in the arms of the man who took it from me—and gave me everything in return.

"Stay with me," I murmur, the words slipping out before I consider them.

His arms tighten around me, lips pressing a kiss to my temple. "I wasn't planning on going anywhere." His voice is warm with affection. "Wild horses couldn't drag me from this bed."

The declaration, simple but sincere, settles something in me. I've never been one to cuddle after sex, always finding some excuse to create distance—a shower, a glass of water, early meetings the next day. With Cole, all I want is to remain exactly where I am, encircled in his strength, my head resting on his chest where I can hear the steady rhythm of his heart.

"That was..." I begin, struggling to find adequate words.

"Mmm," he agrees, understanding without needing the specifics. "It was."

Angel's Peak

CHAPTER 12

THE ANATOMY OF US

We lapse into comfortable silence again, his fingers continuing their gentle exploration of my skin, now with no intent beyond connection.

"How did you get this?" I trace the outline of a scar on his ribs, curious about its origin.

"Fell out of a tree when I was twelve," he explains, noticing my attention. "Caught a branch on the way down. Seventeen stitches."

"Climbing trees at twelve?" I tease, imagining a younger Cole with the same fearless approach to life. "Weren't you a little old for that?"

"Never too old for climbing trees," he counters with a smile I can hear in his voice. "Especially when you're trying to impress Melissa Jenkins, who lived next door and thought I was a 'boring bookworm.'"

I laugh softly, imagining the scene. "Did it work? Were you impressive?"

"Well, the ambulance ride definitely got her attention," he admits ruefully. "Though not in the way I'd hoped."

The casual anecdote reveals another layer of him—the boy

beneath the confident man, the vulnerability beneath the strength. I find myself hungry for more of these glimpses, these pieces of his history that have shaped who he is.

"Any other scars with stories?" I ask, shifting to prop myself on one elbow to see his face.

His smile is warm and indulgent. "A few, but it's your turn. What about this?" His finger traces a thin white line below my left collarbone, barely visible against my olive skin.

"Bicycle accident. Six years old. Went over the handlebars into a rosebush."

His wince is sympathetic. "Ouch."

"I was more upset about ruining my favorite shirt than about the injury," I recall, the memory surprisingly vivid. "My mother was horrified—she's always been squeamish about blood, which is ironic given that both my parents are doctors."

"Ah, so medicine is the family business." His tone is light but interested. "No pressure there, I'm sure."

"None whatsoever," I agree with exaggerated innocence. "Just subtle reminders about legacy and tradition at every family dinner."

He laughs, the sound vibrating through his chest beneath my hand. "And yet you chose trauma surgery—probably the specialty most guaranteed to give your blood-averse mother heart palpitations."

The observation is unexpectedly insightful. "I never thought of it that way," I admit. "But you might be right. There may have been an element of rebellion in my choice."

"Along with genuine aptitude and passion," he adds, not letting me diminish my achievements. "You don't become a department head through rebellion alone."

I smile, appreciating his perspective. "True. I do love what I do, maternal approval notwithstanding."

His hand comes up to brush a strand of hair from my face, the gesture tender in a way that makes my chest tighten. "It shows. When you talk about your work, you light up. It's beautiful to watch."

The simple compliment touches me more deeply than more elaborate praise might have. He sees me—not just the accomplished surgeon or the attractive woman, but the person beneath, with all my passion, drive, and purpose.

"What about you?" I ask, genuinely curious. "Did you always want to be a doctor?"

He considers this, fingers still playing with my hair. "Not always."

"What changed your mind?"

"Funny enough, I shadowed a trauma surgeon during my sophomore year of college," he explains. "Watched him manage six critical patients simultaneously, coordinate with every department in the hospital, advocate fiercely for his patients' needs, and never lose his composure or compassion through a forty-eight-hour shift from hell."

His admiration for this mentor is evident in his voice. "I realized that was the kind of healthcare provider I wanted to be—in the thick of it, hands-on, forming real connections with patients. The direct care, not just the diagnosis and treatment plan."

The insight into his professional choices helps me understand him better—his focus on community, his emphasis on relationship over status, and his comfort with a less prestigious but no less vital role in healthcare.

"You're good at it," I tell him, thinking of how I watched him interact with patients during my brief stay in Angel's Peak. "The connection part, especially. Your patients trust you implicitly."

"I appreciate that." He smiles at the compliment, the kind that lingers in his eyes more than on his lips.

A beat of silence passes. His fingers trail lazily down my spine, not sexual—just there, steady, anchoring.

"But truthfully?" he says, voice dipping quieter. "Med school wasn't even on my radar until I realized the military would pay for it."

"You served?" That catches my attention, and then I vaguely remember him mentioning it the night we met.

"Seven years. Army. They paid for my education. I gave them my time—and then some." His thumb brushes my shoulder absently, his voice steady, matter-of-fact. "I worked on a critical care transport team. We flew into hot zones, stabilized soldiers on the front lines, and got them to a hospital alive. High-intensity trauma, field medicine, no margin for error."

I feel him beneath me—not just the body, but the weight of his past, his purpose.

"That's where I fell in love with emergency medicine," he continues. "Not just because it's fast, but because it matters. It's immediate. Life or death, every minute." His tone doesn't hold bravado. No need to impress. Just truth. "You don't always get long-term outcomes. You don't always get thank-yous. But you get to do something. Right then, right there. Sometimes, that's enough."

"It explains a lot." I lay my head against his chest, listening to the quiet thrum of his heart.

"Like what?"

"Why you're calm under pressure. Why you don't waste time on bullshit. Why you're..." I search for the word. "Solid."

"Solid, huh?" That earns a quiet laugh. "What about dominant?"

"You're that too, in the best way. Steady. Strong. Capable." I tilt my head, grinning.

His arms tighten around me, a subtle pull that says more than words.

"You liked the cuffs," he says, not a question but a knowing statement.

"I did." I nod, pulse skittering.

"And the crop?" His voice dips low, gravel edged with silk. "You didn't expect to like that."

"No," I whisper, throat suddenly dry. "I didn't."

"But you did."

I swallow, then nod again.

"I need to hear it, sweetheart." His hand cups the back of my head, guiding me to look up at him fully. "No hiding. No pretending."

"I liked it," I admit, voice barely more than breath. "The cuffs, the crop... all of it. You made it feel—safe. And intense. And—God—it was so good, better than I ever imagined something like that could be."

"That's because you give everything when you surrender." His eyes soften, even as his grip on me stays firm. "You don't hold back."

"I didn't know I could be like that," I whisper.

"You are like that," he says, brushing his lips across my temple. "And I fucking love it."

I press my face into his throat, overwhelmed by how exposed I feel—how seen. Not just for the polished, in-control surgeon I've always been... but for this other version of me. The one only he has brought out. The one who kneels. Obeys. Burns.

He doesn't pull away. Doesn't tease. Just holds me tighter, skin against skin, the silence between us rich with truth.

"I've got you," he murmurs. "Every side of you. Every scar. Every secret."

With startling clarity I realize how safe I am with him. Not just in the bedroom, but in the world.

His hand squeezes mine, warm and sure. I can feel the calluses on his fingers—earned, not inherited.

"So what made you leave the military?" I turn my head slightly, studying his profile in the dim light.

"Being in the military teaches you to assess fast, act faster, and carry the weight when no one else can," he says softly. "That doesn't go away when the uniform comes off."

"No," I whisper. "It doesn't."

This is what sets him apart. Not just his strength but his willingness to carry others. To step into the chaos and offer calm. His chest rises with a long breath, his thumb tracing idle circles against my skin.

"Seven years is a long time in combat medicine," he says quietly. "I'd seen enough broken bodies. Enough loss. I loved the work, the people—but there comes a point when the weight never fully leaves your shoulders."

He pauses, not for effect, but to gather something heavy before sharing it.

"I didn't want to burn out or become numb. That's how mistakes happen. How compassion dies."

My fingers tighten around his, silent understanding passing between us.

"So you went back to Chicago."

A faint smile pulls at his mouth—wry, nostalgic, tinged with something else.

"Yeah. Took a position at Rush, figured I'd reconnect with family, build a life there."

"You didn't like it." It's not a question.

He shakes his head. "Big hospital. Prestige, politics. And people who measured success in publications and titles, not in lives touched."

There's no bitterness in his voice—just quiet conviction.

"I tried to make it fit," he continues. "But I felt like a cog in a machine. One patient in, one patient out. No time to see them. To know them. And I missed that. The connection. The purpose."

I can almost see it—him walking those sterile halls, shoulders tense, jaw tight, feeling like something vital was slipping away.

"So you came back here," I murmur.

He nods. "Angel's Peak grounded me. It reminded me why I got into medicine in the first place. Not to climb ladders. Not to chase accolades. But to help others." His gaze lifts to mine, intense and unflinching.

His smile is pleased but humble. "It's easier in a small community. You're not just treating the illness or injury—you're treating Mrs. Wilson whose grandchildren you delivered, or Jake Miller who taught you to fish when you first moved to town." He's quiet for a moment, considering the question. "In a place like Angel's Peak, I can practice medicine the way I believe it should be—holistically, personally, without the bureaucracy and politics plaguing larger institutions."

The subtle dig at my world—the urban medical center with its hierarchy and competition—doesn't escape me. But there's no judgment in his tone, just a statement of his values and choices.

"Different approaches, different settings," I observe. "Both valid, both necessary." My chest tightens with something I can't quite name.

Cole didn't return to Angel's Peak for the slower pace. He returned because it gave him back himself, and maybe, just maybe... this place, this man, this moment—Is starting to give something back to me, too.

He must see the question in my eyes, the quiet wondering if a place like Angel's Peak really gives him enough of what he needs.

He tips his head slightly, a small smile tugging at one corner of his mouth.

"And for the record," he says, voice low and knowing, "I still get plenty of trauma experience here."

"Oh?"

His thumb brushes along my knuckles, lazy and warm. "You'd be surprised how many people injure themselves doing stupid shit in the mountains. Backcountry skiers, overconfident climbers, tourists who think they're invincible until they aren't."

I laugh softly.

He smiles, but there's an edge of steel beneath it. "Snowmobile wrecks. Avalanche victims. Hypothermia, concussions, compound fractures miles from the nearest road. When those calls come in, I'm back in it—triage, stabilize, transport. It's like the military in that way. Fast, high-stakes. You do what you can in the moment and get them out alive."

"And the hospital's equipped for that?"

"Not always. We need another doc. Two really."

"Two?"

"A family practitioner and another ER doc or trauma surgeon." His tone is dry. "I've got medevac on speed dial, wilderness kits in my truck, and training that doesn't rely on four walls and perfect conditions."

I look up at him, more impressed than I want to admit.

"It's the best of both worlds," he says simply. "The adrenaline of emergency medicine when it counts... and the quiet, human parts the rest of the time."

I feel it—that same quiet steadiness he's shown me since the beginning. The kind of man who doesn't need to shout his strength because he lives it.

"Exactly." His hand finds mine, fingers intertwining. "The world needs brilliant surgeons in state-of-the-art hospitals just as much as it needs dedicated providers in rural clinics. Different pieces of the same puzzle."

I smile, but my chest tightens.

Because I heard it.

He said trauma surgeon. Not just any doctor. Not just help. He needs someone like me.

And for a heartbeat, I imagine it—trading my long shifts and overrun OR schedules for mountain sunrises, knowing every patient by name, being part of something quieter, more personal.

But it doesn't last.

Because no matter how much I want to give him everything, Angel's Peak isn't built for someone like me. Not long-term. Not professionally.

The trauma center in Denver throws everything at me—multi-vehicle crashes, gunshot wounds, construction accidents, high-stakes surgery that pushes my skills to the edge of exhaustion. I've trained for this. Lived for this. And if I walk away now, I know what happens.

Those skills dull.

Muscle memory fades.

The edge I've earned becomes a memory instead of a blade.

He may need a trauma surgeon—but not *this* trauma surgeon. Not the one who thrives in chaos, who lives for the controlled burn of adrenaline and split-second decisions with lives on the line.

But I don't say any of that aloud.

Because I just want to be—still, quiet and breathe the same air as him. Letting myself pretend, just for a while, that maybe there's a world where we fit without compromise.

"Speaking of puzzles," I say, shifting closer to kiss his jaw, "I think I've figured out one piece."

"Oh?" His eyebrow lifts in question, but his arm tightens around me.

"Mmm." I trail my fingers down his chest, feeling the muscles tighten beneath my touch. "I've determined that your assessment of me earlier—'elegant, accomplished, carefully controlled'—was accurate as far as it went."

"But?" he prompts, catching the implication in my tone.

"But it was incomplete." My hand continues its downward journey, gratified to feel his immediate physical response. "There's another side you bring out in me. One that's not in control at all."

His breath catches as my fingers encircle him. "I've noticed," he manages, voice roughening. "It's becoming one of my favorite things about us."

"Us," I repeat, the simple pronoun somehow significant. "I like the sound of that."

"So do I." He moves suddenly, rolling to position himself above me, his weight supported on his forearms. "And I intend to keep bringing out that *uncontrolled* side of you as often as possible."

His mouth claims mine in a kiss that quickly rekindles the desire I thought momentarily sated. As his hands begin their expert exploration again, as my body responds with increasing urgency to his touch, I surrender to the moment and the connection that continues to grow between us.

Whatever challenges await us—distance, schedules, the competing demands of our respective careers—they can wait. This moment belongs to us, to our discovery of each other, and to the unexpected joy of finding a perfect match in the most unlikely circumstances.

And as Cole proves, yet again, his mastery of my body and his understanding of my deepest desires, I hope that this connection is strong enough to withstand whatever tests lie ahead.

Angel's Peak

CHAPTER 13

MOUNTAIN DECISIONS

THREE MONTHS.

That's how long Cole and I have been making this impossible relationship work. Twelve weekends of driving back and forth between Denver and Angel's Peak, stealing precious days between demanding schedules, and falling asleep with phones pressed to our ears when physical distance couldn't be bridged.

Three months of discovering what began in a snowstorm has grown into something strong enough to weather far greater challenges than mere geography.

I lean against the railing of my balcony, coffee warming my hands in the early morning air as I watch the city below slowly come to life. It's Sunday—my last morning with Cole before he drives back to Angel's Peak, and I dive into a week of administrative meetings and scheduled surgeries.

These moments—the quiet in-between times when we're not making love or making plans—have become precious to me. Time when we exist together, comfortable in shared silence, drawing strength from each other's presence.

The sliding door opens behind me, and I feel him before I see him—the solid warmth of his chest against my back, strong arms encircling my waist, lips pressing a kiss to the side of my neck.

"Morning," Cole murmurs, voice still rough with sleep. "Missed you in bed."

"Sorry." I lean back into his embrace, allowing myself the simple pleasure of being held. "I didn't want to wake you. You were driving late."

His shift ran long yesterday, delayed by a hiking accident that required his attention. He didn't arrive at my apartment until after midnight. He was exhausted but still insistent on making the drive rather than waiting until morning.

"Worth it." He rests his chin on my shoulder to share my view of the city. "Even if it meant missing sunrise with you."

The casual affection in his voice, in his touch, no longer startles me as it once did. I've grown accustomed to this—to being cherished, to being prioritized by someone whose strength matches my own.

"Coffee?" I offer, lifting my mug.

"In a minute." His arms tighten slightly, keeping me close. "I'm enjoying this first."

We stand together in comfortable silence, watching Denver transition from night to day, the early sun glinting off glass and steel. It's a different beauty from the mountain sunrises Cole usually witnesses—man-made rather than natural, ordered rather than wild—but beautiful nonetheless.

"What's on your mind?" he finally asks, always attuned to the subtle shifts in my mood. "You're thinking hard for a Sunday morning."

I consider deflecting, offering some innocuous observation about the weather or upcoming work projects, but one of the many things I've learned in these months with Cole is the value of directness, of saying what needs to be said without hedging or hesitation.

"I got a call yesterday," I begin, turning in his arms to face him. "From Dr. Reid."

Cole's eyebrows lift in surprise. "Angel's Peak's Dr. Reid? My Dr. Reid?"

"His wife's recovery has worsened. They've decided to relocate permanently to Arizona, where their kids can help with her care." I take a breath, delivering the news that could change everything between us. "He's officially retiring. The position is open."

Understanding dawns immediately in those perceptive blue eyes. "And he called you about it? Not me?"

"He called me because the hospital board chair suggested it," I explain. "Your name came up as the obvious choice to replace him permanently, but you've declined twice already."

"I didn't tell you about that." A flash of something—guilt? regret?—crosses his features.

"No, you didn't." There's no accusation in my tone, merely observation.

"I didn't see the point. Taking the full physician position would mean more responsibility, more administrative work, less direct patient care." He sighs, running a hand through his sleep-tousled hair. "All the things I left Chicago to avoid. Not to mention..." His voice trails off, leaving the rest unsaid.

His reasoning makes sense and aligns perfectly with my understanding of his priorities and values. Yet something doesn't quite add up.

"When did they first approach you?" I ask, unable to keep the edge of professional curiosity from creeping into my voice. I'm still a diagnostician at heart, always searching for the missing piece that completes the clinical picture.

"The first time was before I met you," he says, confirming my suspicion. "The second was about a month ago."

A month.

I take a slow sip of my now-cooling coffee, letting the timeline settle.

"Right around the time we started talking about making this relationship more..." I hesitate, not because I don't know the word—but because I do. "*Defined.*"

His expression doesn't flicker. He knows exactly what I mean.

Not exclusivity. Not dating. But structure. Control. The kind of dominance that doesn't stop when the clothes come off.

He doesn't deny it. Just holds my gaze, steady and unflinching, waiting for me to catch up. And suddenly, I do.

"You didn't take it because of me."

The words leave me on a breath. "Because accepting would've tied you more firmly to Angel's Peak. It would've made the distance harder to bridge. Harder for us."

The implications spread like wildfire.

This wasn't just a missed opportunity or a professional choice.

It was a sacrifice.

And he made it for me.

Cole's expression doesn't soften, but something shifts in his eyes—resolve surfacing beneath the steady calm.

"I made that decision after we talked about." His voice is low, sure. Not dramatic. Just true. "I couldn't ask for that— couldn't lead you through that—if I was still living hours away, tied to a town you'd have no reason to stay in." He leans forward slightly, eyes locked on mine.

"Cole..." I reach for him, and he takes my hand, lifting it to his mouth for a kiss. "You didn't...you don't have to do that."

"If we're going to *define* this... then I *need to* be with you. In your life. Your space. Not as a visitor. But as the man who puts you on your knees at night and kisses your forehead before work in the morning."

My heart stutters, caught between breath and surrender.

"I want *us*, and if that means walking away from Angel's Peak, I'm willing to do that. I'm heere to fight for what matters."

Me.

Us.

Every word lands like a vow.

"Cole." I set my mug on the railing, raising both hands to frame his face. "You can't make career decisions based on what might or might not happen with us."

"Why not?" he challenges, covering my hands with his own. "You're more important to me than a title or a paycheck. If there's even a chance that taking that position would create another obstacle between us, it's not worth it. Not to mention, I couldn't even think of accepting it when I was planning on moving to Denver."

The declaration, delivered with his characteristic straight-forwardness, both warms and troubles me.

"That's not how this works," I insist gently. "We each need to make professional choices that fulfill us and align with our values and goals. Otherwise, resentment builds. Trust me, I've seen it happen."

"Is that what this is about?" His expression shifts to concern. "Are you feeling resentful of the compromises you've been making for us?"

"No," I assure him quickly. "That's not it at all. But I need to know you're making decisions for the right reasons, not sacrificing opportunities you might want because of logistical challenges in our relationship."

He studies me for a long moment, his gaze so intent I feel he's seeing straight through to my deepest thoughts. "Why did Reid call you and not me?" he finally asks, returning to the original thread. "What *exactly* did he want?"

This is the part I've been circling around, the revelation that could change everything.

"He wanted to gauge my interest in the position." I watch Cole's expression carefully. "Or rather, the board chair did, through him."

For a moment, he doesn't seem to process my words. Then understanding dawns, his eyes widening slightly. "They're offering you Dr. Reid's job? They want you to come to Angel's Peak as a trauma surgeon?"

I nod, my pulse quickening as I voice the possibility aloud. "They want a trauma-qualified physician to expand the clinic's emergency capabilities. Apparently, tourism has increased enough to justify a higher level of care, especially for mountain accidents."

"But your position at Denver General," he begins, brow furrowing. "The department head role you worked so hard for..."

"Would need to be sacrificed," I finish for him. "Yes."

"Well, that's not happening." He shakes his head, stepping back slightly though his hands remain on my arms. "If one of us is moving, it's me. That's your dream job. Everything you've worked toward."

"It *was* my dream," I gently correct. "For the longest time, I thought it was. So much so, that it *defined* me. Blinded me. I couldn't see what was important."

"What are you saying?" He searches my face, looking for signs of doubt or hesitation.

"I'm saying the past three months have changed me." The words come easier than I expected. "Changed what I want, what I value, and what I see in my future."

"Because of me?" His voice holds a note of caution, of concern that I might be making decisions based on emotion rather than reason—the very thing he just admitted to doing.

"Partly because of you—of us," I acknowledge. "But not

entirely. The department head position hasn't been what I expected. More politics than medicine, more meetings than mentoring. I'm spending my days on budgets and staffing disputes instead of doing the work I love. My OR time is half what it was."

It's a truth I've been reluctant to admit, even to myself. The prestigious position I fought so hard to achieve has proved to be more of a burden than a blessing, taking me further from patients and procedures and the hands-on healing that drew me to medicine in the first place.

"You never said anything," Cole observes, no judgment in his tone. "Why didn't you say something?"

"I didn't want to admit it. To you, or myself. More to myself." I smile ruefully. "Pride, I guess. After all that talk about career ambitions and professional goals, it seemed weak to confess that the summit I worked so hard to climb wasn't what I hoped for."

"It's not weak to reassess. It's wise." His expression softens, understanding replacing concern. "Goals should evolve as we do."

The simple acceptance in his words, the absence of any 'I told you so' about the potential emptiness of corporate advancement, reminds me yet again why I've fallen for this man. His strength lies not in domination but in support, his confidence not in being right but in being real.

"So," he says after a moment, carefully neutral. "Are you considering this offer?"

"I'm considering a lot of things," I admit. "Including what moving to Angel's Peak would mean for us. For our future."

Something flares in his eyes at the word 'future'—hope, maybe, or caution.

"What do you think it would mean?" He gives me space to articulate my thoughts rather than presuming.

I take a deep breath, organizing the swirl of possibilities

coherently. "It would mean no more three-hour drives. No more snatched weekends and exhausted Monday mornings. No more falling asleep on the phone because we're too tired to talk but too attached to hang up."

"Those are the things it would eliminate," he notes. "What about what it would create?"

The question is perfect, forcing me to look beyond the logistical benefits to the deeper implications. "It would create... possibility," I say slowly. "Space for us to grow together without the strain of distance. Opportunity to build something real, something lasting. To move forward with..."

His hands tighten on my arms, hope more evident now in his expression. "Is that what you want? Something real and lasting with me?"

The vulnerability in his question pierces straight to my heart. This strong, confident man who commands every room he enters, who takes charge so naturally in every situation—he's asking for reassurance, for confirmation that I see the same future he does.

The question is simple. But the weight behind it is anything but.

I swallow, my gaze dropping to where his fingers grip my arms—firm, grounding, safe. A thousand thoughts clamor for airtime. The move. The shift in careers. The redefinition of everything I thought I wanted.

And something else.

Something darker. Deeper.

The part of me that aches from his crop. That pulses at the memory of his voice telling me to burn for him. That wants to kneel...

"I want..." The words stall in my throat, not because they're untrue, but because they're too raw. Too revealing.

His thumb brushes the inside of my elbow, coaxing, but I'm not ready.

"I want to keep exploring this," I say instead, the safest truth I can give him. "Whatever this is becoming between us. I don't have the right language for all of it yet, but—"

My breath hitches. I force myself to look up.

"I know I don't want to lose it."

Something flickers across his face—recognition. Maybe even understanding.

He doesn't press.

He just nods once, slow and sure, his voice a low promise.

"What's that?"

"Everything. And we're just getting started." His smile starts slow but grows into something brilliant, transforming his already handsome face into something that takes my breath away. "Well then," he says, hands sliding up to cup my face, voice thick with affection and heat, "what are we talking about?"

"I think I'm quitting my job."

The words land between us, raw and real. His eyes search mine, and for a heartbeat, neither of us breathes.

Then—his thumb sweeps over my cheek, and his voice drops. "Tess, I want you to sit on this. Give it a really good think. Whatever you decide, I'm behind you, one hundred percent. Whether you quit and join me in Angel's Peak, or I quit and join you down here, I want us to be together. You're worth it."

"The role is not just trauma surgeon, but Medical Director. I'm going to make this move—Angel's Peak, us—I need to know we're walking in with clear eyes. That you're okay with me stepping into a role where I'm your boss. Would you be comfortable with me taking the lead role? With the dynamics that would create?"

"Have I ever given you the impression I have a problem with strong, capable women?" His laugh is low and intimate, pure heat wrapped in velvet. "Besides, I'm not interested in the bureaucratic bullshit. I turned that job down before we even met."

One hand slides into my hair, cradling the back of my head in that now-familiar gesture of gentle possession.

"Besides," he adds, his gaze darkening with promise, "we've established pretty clearly that professional hierarchies have nothing to do with what happens behind closed doors—our bedroom or otherwise."

The reminder of our private dynamic sends a pleasant shiver through me. In the months we've been together, we've perfected that balance—my leadership in professional settings, his in intimate ones, each of us secure enough to yield control in the appropriate context.

"There's still a lot to consider," I caution, not wanting to rush such a significant decision. "My parents will think I'm throwing away my career. The Denver medical community will see it as a step backward. And Angel's Peak is so different from anything I've known..."

"All true," he agrees, not dismissing my concerns. "And yet I've watched you these past months. You light up when you talk about the cases at my clinic—the direct impact, the personal connection with patients. You come alive in Angel's Peak in a way I don't see in Denver."

His observation strikes me with its accuracy. The weekends I've spent in his mountain town, occasionally helping out at the clinic when needs arose, have been among my most fulfilling recent professional experiences. The simplicity of treating patients and knowing the people behind the medical charts—it's rekindled something in me that I didn't realize had been fading.

"I still need time to think it through and weigh all the factors."

"Of course, and I wouldn't let you make such a big decision without time to really think it through." He tucks a strand of hair behind my ear, his touch infinitely tender. "While I can't make this decision for you, I can certainly order you to take the proper time to weigh all the possibilities."

The words settle over me slowly. Not pushy. Not presumptuous. But firm. Intentional.

A command wrapped in care.

And it lands differently than I expect—like a balm rather than a burden.

Because it's not about the decision. It's about the process. About making sure I don't rush, don't crumble under pressure. That I hold space for myself the way he already does.

A flicker of heat stirs low in my belly, not from lust but from something deeper. Recognition. Of what this is becoming. Of who he is when he takes control—not to limit me, but to protect my bandwidth, my energy, my worth.

I look up at him, heart thudding in a steady, dangerous rhythm.

"That sounded a lot like an order," I murmur.

His smile is slow. Unapologetic. "It was."

My body responds to the quiet authority threading his voice. He already knows how much I like it.

The weight of our words settles over me like a blanket, warming places I didn't know were cold. Whatever I decide about the job, Cole will be there—supporting, encouraging, and loving me through it.

"I love you," I say, the declaration simpler and more natural than I expected. "Whatever I decide about Angel's Peak, whatever challenges we face—that won't change."

For a moment, he seems stunned, those expressive blue eyes widening in surprise before softening with an emotion so deep it makes my chest ache.

"Tess." Just my name, but the way he says it—like a prayer, like a promise—tells me everything. His hands frame my face with exquisite gentleness. "I've been in love with you since that first snowstorm. Since you walked into my clinic and challenged every plan I had for my life."

The admission, delivered with his characteristic directness, fills me with a joy so pure it borders on pain.

"Why didn't you say something sooner?" I ask, though I already know the answer.

"Because you needed to find your own way to it," he says. "Because I knew when the words came, they'd be real. Worth waiting for."

And then he's kissing me, his mouth claiming mine with a tenderness that quickly deepens into passion. I yield to him willingly, arms winding around his neck as his hands slide down to pull me firmly against him. The taste of him—now familiar but no less intoxicating—sends heat spiraling through me, driving away the morning chill.

When we finally part, both slightly breathless, I rest my forehead against his chest, feeling the steady beat of his heart beneath my cheek. His arms remain around me, solid and secure, a physical echo of the emotional certainty building between us.

"Whatever you decide about the job," he murmurs against my hair, "we'll make it work. If you stay in Denver, I'll move. If you come to Angel's Peak, I'll spend every day showing you why it should be our home."

Home.

The word resonates through me, carrying echoes of possibility I hadn't allowed myself to consider until now. Not a place to live or work, but somewhere to belong, to build a life, to create a future with the person who has so unexpectedly become essential to my happiness.

"I think," I say slowly, the clarity of certainty beginning to form, "that I need to visit Angel's Peak again. Soon. To talk with the board, to see the clinic with fresh eyes. To imagine what a life there might look like."

His smile is warm against my temple. "I can arrange that. Though I should warn you—once you start imagining your life in Angel's Peak with me, it going to be impossible to imagine being anywhere else."

"Is that what happened to you?" I ask, curious about his journey to the place that's become so central to his identity. "When did you know it was home, not just an escape?"

He considers this, his expression thoughtful. "There wasn't one moment. More a series of realizations. The first time a patient brought me homemade soup when I caught the flu. The day I finished building my cabin deck and stood looking at the mountain view, feeling like I'd finally found where I belonged. The morning I realized I no longer thought of Chicago as 'back home' but just as 'Chicago.'"

His description paints a picture of gradual belonging, of roots growing slowly but deeply into unfamiliar soil until they become anchored enough to withstand any storm. It's a different path than my own—all careful planning and deliberate achievement—but no less valid and no less fulfilling.

"And now?" I prompt, wanting to hear the end of the story, how he views his mountain home now that our lives have become so entwined.

His eyes find mine, open and honest as always. "Now I look at Angel's Peak and see not just my past and present, but our future, if you want it."

Then, with a mischievous glint and a grin that's pure trouble, he adds, "And yeah... I might also picture how incredible you'll look tied to our bed, begging me to let you come."

I laugh, breathless and already flushed. Because, of course, he can't help himself.

There are still logistics to consider, details to arrange, and practical matters to resolve. But in this moment, with the morning sun warming my skin and Cole's love warming my heart, the decision feels less daunting than it did minutes ago.

But I'm not letting him have the last word.

"Mmhmm." I stretch languidly, a wicked smile tugging at my lips. "If you're thinking about tying me up… There's no time like the present."

"Sweetheart, challenge accepted." He growls low in his throat, the sound reverberating straight through me.

As his lips find mine again, as his arms create a haven of strength and tenderness around me, I allow myself to fully embrace the truth that's been growing these past months: sometimes the detours in life—the unexpected snowstorms, the chance encounters, the paths we never planned to take—lead us exactly where we need to be.

LOVE THE HEAT, DANGER, AND HEART IN ANGEL'S Peak?

Get ready to hike higher, fall harder, and surrender deeper…

Up next: Rescued by the Mountain Guide

When ambitious travel writer Cloe Matthews heads into the Rockies for a career-making article, she doesn't expect to be stranded—or saved by Jackson Hart, the grumpy, guarded mountain man with ice in his veins and hands that know exactly how to melt her.

But when a blizzard traps them together in his one-room mountain shelter, sparks fly fast and hot—and something wild and undeniable ignites between them.

HE'S USED TO SAVING LIVES. NOT SURRENDERING his heart.

   Grumpy/Sunshine
   Forced proximity

- 🔥 *One bed*
- 🔥 *Dominant hero*
- 🔥 *Emotional walls torn down*
- 🔥 *Trapped in a snowstorm*
- 🔥 *Wounded alpha with a tragic past*

DON'T MISS WHAT HAPPENS NEXT IN ANGEL'S Peak—where passion is raw, the mountains are unforgiving, and love comes when you least expect it.

Read: Rescued by the Mountain Guide

————

Angel's Peak

CHAPTER 14

EPILOGUE

PEAK HAPPINESS

One Year Later

"Dr. Carrington, you have a call on line two."

I glance up from the patient chart I'm reviewing, smiling at our receptionist through the open door of my office. "Thanks, Jenny. I'll take it."

The Angel's Peak Medical Clinic has changed significantly in the twelve months since I accepted the position as Medical Director. What was once a single exam room with basic equipment has expanded to include a proper emergency bay, updated diagnostic technology, and a small but well-equipped surgical suite for traumas and minor procedures. Tourism has boomed, and with it, the need for more comprehensive medical care in this remote mountain community.

I pick up the phone, already knowing who's calling. "Dr. Carrington speaking."

"Hello, Doctor." Cole's deep voice sends a familiar warmth through me, even after all this time. "Just checking if we're still on for lunch."

"Wouldn't miss it," I assure him, glancing at the clock. "Meet you at the cabin in twenty minutes?"

"Perfect. I've got something special planned."

The promise in his tone makes my pulse quicken. "I'm intrigued."

"Good. See you soon." His chuckle is low and intimate.

I hang up, unable to suppress a smile as I finish my notes and gather my things. A year into our life together and Cole still affects me like no one else ever has—or ever will.

The decision to leave Denver was the hardest yet easiest decision of my life. It was hard because I walked away from the prestige and career I had spent years building. It was easy because with each visit to Angel's Peak, with each moment spent in the clinic and the community, I felt more confident this was where I belonged.

My parents were predictably horrified. "Throwing away your career for a man," my mother lamented as if I were some lovesick teenager rather than a respected surgeon making a considered professional choice.

It took months for them to understand I wasn't abandoning medicine but embracing a different way to practice it —one that brought me closer to patients and to the fundamental healing that had drawn me to the field in the first place. Their first visit to Angel's Peak, seeing the clinic I was building and the life I was creating, finally changed their perspective.

The mountain air is crisp as I step outside, and autumn paints the surrounding peaks in brilliant golds and reds. I breathe deeply, still marveling at the absence of city pollution and the clarity of mountain oxygen filling my lungs.

My car—a sensible SUV now, better suited to mountain living than my sleek city sedan—waits in the clinic's small parking lot. The drive to our cabin takes less than ten minutes, and the winding road is now as familiar to me as my reflection.

Our cabin.

The thought still gives me a small thrill. Cole suggested I move in with him immediately, but I insisted on renting my own place first, needing to establish my independence in this new community.

That resolution lasted precisely six days before we acknowledged the absurdity of maintaining separate homes when we spent every night together anyway. The small cabin Cole built on the mountainside, with its spectacular views and rustic charm, became our shared sanctuary.

Pulling into the driveway, Cole's truck is already parked outside. Smoke curls invitingly from the chimney.

Inside, the scent of pine and wood smoke greets me, along with something delicious simmering on the stove. "Cole?"

"Out here," his voice calls from the deck.

I drop my bag and make my way through the cabin to the back deck, where a breathtaking view of the valley spreads below. Cole stands at the railing, broad shoulders outlined against the mountain backdrop. He turns at my approach, and the smile that spreads across his face still makes my heart skip.

"Right on time," he says, crossing to pull me into his arms. His kiss is warm and familiar, yet no less exciting for its familiarity. "Hungry?"

"Starving," I admit, leaning into his solid strength. "Morning clinic was packed. Three broken bones from a school field trip gone wrong, plus Mrs. Henderson convinced she's caught some exotic disease from her Caribbean cruise."

"Let me guess—internet diagnosis?"

"Of course. Took twenty minutes to convince her she has a simple sinus infection, not dengue fever."

He laughs, the sound vibrating through his chest against my cheek. "And they say rural medicine isn't exciting."

I pull back to look up at him, drinking in the strong lines of his face, the blue eyes that see straight through to my core. "Never a dull moment. Especially not with you."

"Speaking of which," he says, taking my hand to lead me back inside, "I've got some news."

The table is already set for lunch, a bottle of champagne chilling in an ice bucket catching my attention immediately. "Champagne with lunch on a Wednesday? What are we celebrating?"

Cole's expression is a mixture of excitement and satisfaction as he pulls out my chair. "The board approved our proposal. Full funding for the emergency transport program. Helicopter pad construction starts next month."

"Cole!" I launch myself into his arms, beyond professional decorum in my excitement. "That's incredible! We've been working on that proposal for months!"

The emergency helicopter program had been my most ambitious goal since taking over the clinic—a dedicated transport system to get critical patients from our remote location to larger hospitals when necessary. The funding seemed like a long shot, given the costs involved.

"They were impressed with the case statistics you compiled," he says, holding me tight against him. "And the letters of support from other regional hospitals didn't hurt."

"We did it," I breathe, the victory sweeter for being shared. "We really did it."

"You did it," he corrects, tucking a strand of hair behind my ear. "Your reputation, your expertise, your determination. I just provided moral support and occasional editing."

"Partnership," I counter firmly. "Equal credit."

His smile softens, something deeper than professional pride shining in his eyes. "Partner," he agrees, the word carrying layers of meaning beyond our working relationship.

He pours the champagne, handing me a flute with a formality that seems almost ceremonial. "To the Angel's Peak Emergency Medical Transport Program," he toasts. "And to the brilliant, beautiful doctor who made it happen."

We clink glasses, sipping the crisp bubbles as satisfaction settles over me. This—the achievement, the forward progress, the knowledge that we're genuinely improving care for this community—fills a place in my soul that prestigious titles and corner offices never could.

"I have one more piece of news." Cole sets down his glass with deliberate care. "Something I wanted to discuss with you before making a final decision."

"What is it? Is everything okay?" The sudden seriousness in his tone makes me pay closer attention.

"More than okay." He takes my hand across the table, thumb tracing circles on my palm in that familiar gesture that never fails to center me. "Denver General called yesterday. They're expanding their rural medicine outreach program, looking for experienced providers to help train city doctors rotating through rural settings."

"And they want you," I guess, understanding immediately why this would appeal to him. Cole has always been an excellent teacher. He's patient and insightful with the medical students and residents we occasionally host.

He nods. "It would mean traveling to Denver once or twice a month for a few days, then hosting their doctors here for hands-on experience. Good pay, flexible scheduling around our clinic needs."

"It sounds perfect for you," I say honestly. "You'd be an incredible teacher for city doctors who've never experienced rural healthcare challenges."

"You're not concerned about me being away a few days each month?" he asks, studying my expression carefully.

I squeeze his hand, touched by his consideration but sure in my response. "We spent months commuting between cities. A few days apart now and then is nothing—especially when you're doing something so meaningful."

The relief in his smile tells me he'd already wanted to

accept but needed to ensure I was comfortable with the arrangement. This, too, is part of what makes us work so well together—the constant consideration, the unwillingness to make significant decisions without consultation, the genuine desire for the other's happiness alongside our own.

"Besides," I add with a smile, "absence makes the heart grow fonder, right? I'll have to make sure your homecomings are especially memorable...Sir."

His eyes darken at the suggestion, his thumb pressing more firmly against my palm. "Is that a promise, Dr. Carrington?"

"Absolutely," I assure him, heat building between us across the table. "In fact, we could start practicing those homecomings right now. Lunch can wait, can't it?"

In answer, he stands, pulling me up from my chair and into his arms in one smooth motion. "It can definitely wait."

His mouth claims mine with a hunger that never fails to thrill me, his hands sliding down to lift me effortlessly against him. I wrap my legs around his waist, arms twining around his neck as he carries me toward our bedroom with the same confident strength he brings to everything.

"I've been thinking about this all morning," he murmurs against my neck, laying me on our bed with surprising gentleness given the urgency in his touch.

I reach for the buttons of his shirt.

"Uh-uh, you know the rules." His hand catches mine, stopping my progress with gentle firmness. "Let me." His voice drops to that commanding register that never fails to send heat straight to my core. "Do I need to remind you what we have here?"

His natural dominance is always balanced by profound respect, and my surrender is freely given rather than demanded.

"No, sir." I let my hands fall to my sides in a gesture of willing compliance.

His smile is equal parts tenderness and heat as he undresses me with deliberate care, each button of my blouse undone with tantalizing slowness, each newly revealed inch of skin blessed with his lips or fingertips. By the time he slides the fabric from my shoulders, I'm already breathing heavily, skin flushed with anticipation.

My skirt follows, then the rest, until I lie naked before him while he remains fully clothed—a power imbalance that would once have made me uncomfortable but now only heightens my arousal. There is freedom in this surrender, a liberation in placing myself entirely in his capable hands.

"Beautiful," he murmurs, eyes traveling over me with unhurried appreciation. "Even more beautiful than the first time I saw you like this."

His hand traces a path from my throat to my breast, thumb circling the nipple until it pebbles beneath his touch. When he replaces his fingers with his mouth, hot and wet around the sensitive peak, I arch into the contact, a soft moan escaping me.

"That's it," he encourages, lifting his head to watch my face. "Let me hear you. No holding back. Not with me."

The instruction—for his words are always instructions in moments like these, never merely suggestions—taps into the dynamic we've perfected over our months together. In the clinic, I lead; in our bed, he commands. The balance works because we find profound satisfaction in our respective roles.

He continues his methodical exploration, hands and mouth mapping my body as if committing every curve and hollow to memory. When his fingers finally slide between my thighs, finding me already wet and wanting, his approving growl vibrates against my skin.

"Always so ready for me," he says, the pride in his voice sending another pulse of heat through me. "So perfect."

His touch is expert after months of learning exactly how to please me—where to press, when to stroke, and what rhythm will build my pleasure most effectively. Soon, I'm writhing beneath his hand, hips rising to meet each deliberate caress, breath coming in short gasps as tension coils tighter low in my belly.

"Cole," I plead, beyond pride or restraint. "Please."

"Please what?" he prompts, the question familiar from countless encounters. "Tell me what you need."

"You," I manage, finding words through the haze of mounting pleasure. "Inside me. Now."

He smiles, the expression predatory and tender all at once. "Since you asked so nicely."

Only then does he undress, revealing the body I know as intimately as my own—broad shoulders, muscled chest, narrow hips, powerful thighs. His arousal is evident, impressive, and familiar, a promise of pleasure to come.

When he covers me with his body, the weight and heat of him is exactly what I need—grounding, commanding, perfectly balanced between restraint and urgency. He positions himself between my thighs, the blunt pressure of him teasing my entrance.

"Look at me," he instructs, waiting until my eyes meet his. "I want to watch you take my cock."

The deliberate crudeness of his language, so at odds with his usual articulate speech, sends a fresh surge of heat through me. This, too, is part of our dynamic—the freedom to be raw, primal, and uninhibited in ways we rarely allow ourselves outside this sanctuary we've created.

When he finally enters me, it's in one long, controlled thrust that fills me completely. We groan in unison at the sensation, the perfect joining that never fails to feel like coming home.

"Mine," he growls against my throat, beginning to move with deliberate power. "Say it, Tess. Tell me who you belong to."

"I'm yours, sir," I breathe, admitting both surrender and triumph. "Only yours."

His rhythm increases at my words, each thrust deeper, more purposeful than the last. One hand slides beneath me, lifting my hips to change the angle, driving him even deeper. The new position sends him against that perfect spot inside me with every movement, building pleasure so intense it borders on unbearable.

"Come for me," he commands, his control visibly slipping as his own release approaches. "Let me feel you come around me."

The combination of physical stimulation and verbal command pushes me over the edge. I shatter beneath him, around him, waves of pleasure radiating outward from where we're joined to consume my entire being. His name falls from my lips in a litany, a prayer, a promise.

He follows moments later, rhythm faltering as his release claims him. In that moment of abandon—the only time his careful control entirely slips—I glimpse the depth of his vulnerability and trust in me to witness him so completely undone.

Afterward, he gathers me against him, my head resting on his chest where I can hear the gradual slowing of his heartbeat. His fingers trace idle patterns on my back, touch now soothing rather than arousing.

"I love you," he murmurs against my hair, the words simple but profound. "More than I knew was possible to love another person."

"I love you too," I reply, meaning it with every fiber of my being. "Thank you for showing me what was possible. For helping me find this life I never knew I wanted."

He shifts slightly, reaching into the bedside drawer. "Speaking of which," he says, a new note in his voice drawing my attention. "There's something I've been wanting to ask you."

When I raise my head to look at him, he's holding a small velvet box, open to reveal a stunning ring—a single diamond set in a band that appears to be carved wood inlaid with gold.

"I made the band," he explains, answering my unspoken question. "From the maple I used for our cabin's mantle. So you'd always carry a piece of our home with you."

Tears spring to my eyes at the thoughtfulness, the perfect symbolism of the gesture. "Cole..."

"Tess Carrington," he continues, voice steady despite the emotion shimmering in his eyes. "This year with you has been the most fulfilling of my life. You challenge me, support me, make me better in every way. Will you marry me? Make this official in every sense?"

Though we've spoken of marriage, imagined it in the quiet in-between moments of our lives, hearing the question spoken aloud—with that fierce certainty only he possesses—still steals my breath.

"Yes," I say without hesitation. Joy rises like a tide. "Of course, yes."

His smile is radiant as he slides the ring onto my finger—a smooth, polished band of warm wood encircling a brilliant diamond, the light catching in prismatic flares. It's unconventional, thoughtful, and unmistakably him.

The kiss that follows is deep with promise and soft with reverence. It is not just a celebration but a vow.

When he pulls back, he doesn't let go of my hand.

"There's one more thing."

From his jacket, he pulls a second box—smaller. Velvet. Black.

He opens it to reveal something that steals my breath a second time.

A slender, solid gold chain gleams softly in the afternoon light. At its center rests a delicate but unmistakable heart-shaped lock. Hanging beside it on a fine chain is a tiny key.

His voice is low and reverent.

"This is a symbol of trust. Of everything we are when it's just the two of us. You've given me your heart, your body, and your submission—this is me promising to protect all of it."

He lifts it carefully, its weight glittering between his fingers.

"Will you wear it for me?" His gaze holds mine. Steady. Unflinching. "Not just in private. But always."

My chest tightens, tears stinging the backs of my eyes. Because this isn't just about claiming—it's about cherishing.

"Yes, Sir," I whisper. "Always."

His fingers brush the back of my neck as he fastens the collar in place. The gold warms instantly against my skin. When the tiny lock clicks closed, I feel it all the way through me—a tether, a vow, a promise fulfilled.

He kisses me again. Deeper this time. More possessive. More complete.

Then it hits.

I'm his.

Utterly and unquestionably *his*.

Later, wrapped in the quilt his grandmother made, we stand on the deck, watching the sun begin its descent toward the mountain peaks. Cole's arms encircle me from behind, my head resting against his chest, my newly adorned hand covered by his larger one.

"Happy?" he asks simply.

I consider the question, taking stock of all we've built

together—the thriving clinic serving a community I've grown to love, the cabin that's become a true home, the partnership professional and personal that fulfills me in ways I never anticipated.

"Completely," I answer with absolute certainty. "You?"

"More than I ever thought possible." His arms tighten around me, lips pressing a kiss to my temple.

As the sun gilds the mountains in golden light, as the life we've chosen spreads before us in all its beauty and possibility, I send silent thanks to the snowstorm that forced me off course a year ago. What seemed like misfortune was destiny in disguise.

The detour that led me not *away* from my path but *toward* it—toward Cole, toward Angel's Peak, toward happiness more complete than any I could have planned for myself.

Sometimes, it seems, you have to get lost before you can truly be found. And sometimes, the greatest adventure begins with a wrong turn in a snowstorm, leading you not to shelter for a night but to home for a lifetime.

Home isn't a place, but about the person who makes anywhere feel like it's exactly where you belong.

———

LOVE THE HEAT, DANGER, AND HEART IN ANGEL'S Peak?

Get ready to hike higher, fall harder, and surrender deeper...

Up next: Rescued by the Mountain Guide

When ambitious travel writer Cloe Matthews heads into the Rockies for a career-making article, she doesn't expect to be stranded—or saved by Jackson Hart, the grumpy, guarded mountain man with ice in his veins and hands that know exactly how to melt her.

But when a blizzard traps them together in his one-room mountain shelter, sparks fly fast and hot—and something wild and undeniable ignites between them.

HE'S USED TO SAVING LIVES. NOT SURRENDERING his heart.

- *Grumpy/Sunshine*
- *Forced proximity*
- *One bed*
- *Dominant hero*
- *Emotional walls torn down*
- *Trapped in a snowstorm*
- *Wounded alpha with a tragic past*

DON'T MISS WHAT HAPPENS NEXT IN ANGEL'S Peak—where passion is raw, the mountains are unforgiving, and love comes when you least expect it.

Read: Rescued by the Mountain Guide

Angel's Peak

Please consider leaving a review

I hope you enjoyed this book as much as I enjoyed writing it. If you like this book, please leave a review. I love reviews. I love reading your reviews, and they help other readers decide if this book is worth their time and money. I hope you think it is and decide to share this story with others. A sentence is all it takes. Thank you in advance!

Click on the link below to leave your review
Goodreads
Amazon
Bookbub

Angel's Peak

ELLZ BELLZ

Ellie's Facebook Reader Group

If you are interested in joining the ELLZ BELLZ, Ellie's Facebook reader group, we'd love to have you.

Join Ellie's ELLZ BELLZ.
The ELLZ BELLZ Facebook Reader Group

Sign up for Ellie's Newsletter.
Elliemasters.com/newslettersignup

Also by Ellie Masters

The LIGHTER SIDE

Ellie Masters is the lighter side of the Jet & Ellie Masters writing duo! You will find Contemporary Romance, Military Romance, Romantic Suspense, Billionaire Romance, and Rock Star Romance in Ellie's Works.

YOU CAN FIND ELLIE'S BOOKS HERE:

ELLIEMASTERS.COM/BOOKS

SUGGESTED READING ORDER

START HERE

Rockstar Romance

The Angel Fire Rock Romance Series

EACH BOOK IN THIS SERIES CAN BE READ AS A STANDALONE AND IS ABOUT A DIFFERENT COUPLE WITH AN HEA. IT IS RECOMMENDED THEY ARE READ IN ORDER.

Heart's Insanity

Ashes to New

Heart's Desire

Heart's Collide

Hearts Divided

Hearts Entwined

Forest's FALL

Hearts The Last Beat

CONTINUE HERE...

Rescuing Malia

Rescuing Ally

Delta Team (Coming Soon)

Rescuing Ember

Rescuing Aria

STANDALONES IN THE GUARDIAN HOSTAGE RESCUE SERIES YOU CAN READ ANYTIME

Military Romance

Guardian Personal Protection Specialists

Sybil's Protector

Lyra's Protector

Angel Peak Steamy Instalove Novella Series

(Small Town)

By Ellie Masters

EACH BOOK IN THIS SERIES CAN BE READ AS A STANDALONE AND IS ABOUT A DIFFERENT COUPLE WITH AN HEA.

SNOWED IN WITH THE MOUNTAIN DOCTOR

Rescued by the Mountain Guide

Stranded with the Resort Owner

Matched with the Small-Town Chef

Trapped with the Forest Ranger

Snowbound with the Vineyard Owner

Reunited with the Hometown Hero

The One I Want Series

(Small Town, Military Heroes)

By Jet & Ellie Masters

Michelle

Ivy

HOT READS

Becoming His Series

THIS SERIES MUST BE READ IN ORDER.

The Ballet

Learning to Breathe

Becoming His

Dark Captive Romance

A STANDALONE NOVEL.

She's *MINE*

Angel's Peak

BOOKS BY JET MASTERS

If you enjoyed this book by Ellie Masters, the LIGHTER SIDE of the Jet & Ellie writing duo, and aren't afraid of edgier writing, you might enjoy reading BDSM themed books written by Jet, the DARKER SIDE of the Masters' Writing Team.

The DARKER SIDE
Jet Masters is the darker side of the Jet & Ellie writing duo!

Romantic Suspense
Changing Roles Series:
THIS SERIES MUST BE READ IN ORDER.
Command Me
Control Me
Collar Me
Embracing FATE
Seizing FATE
Accepting FATE

HOT READS

A STANDALONE NOVEL.
Down the Rabbit Hole

Light BDSM Romance
The Ties that Bind

EACH BOOK IN THIS SERIES CAN BE READ AS A STANDALONE AND IS ABOUT A DIFFERENT COUPLE WITH AN HEA.
Alexa
Penny
Michelle
Ivy

HOT READS
Becoming His Series

THIS SERIES MUST BE READ IN ORDER.
The Ballet
Learning to Breathe
Becoming His

Dark Captive Romance

A STANDALONE NOVEL.
She's MINE

About the Author

Ellie Masters is a USA Today Bestselling author and Amazon Top 15 Author who writes Angsty, Steamy, Heart-Stopping, Pulse-Pounding, Can't-Stop-Reading Romantic Suspense. In addition, she's a wife, military mom, doctor, and retired Colonel. She writes romantic suspense filled with all your sexy, swoon-worthy alpha men. Her writing will tug at your heart-strings and leave your heart racing.

Born in the South, raised under the Hawaiian sun, Ellie has traveled the globe while in service to her country. The love of her life, her amazing husband, is her number one fan and biggest supporter. And yes! He's read every word she's written.

She has lived all over the United States—east, west, north, south and central—but grew up under the Hawaiian sun. She's also been privileged to have lived overseas, experiencing other cultures and making lifelong friends. Now, Ellie is proud to call herself a Southern transplant, learning to say y'all and "bless her heart" with the best of them.

Ellie's favorite way to spend an evening is curled up on a couch, laptop in place, watching a fire, drinking a good wine, and bringing forth all the characters from her mind to the page and hopefully into the hearts of her readers.

FOR MORE INFORMATION
elliemasters.com

facebook.com/elliemastersromance

x.com/Ellie__Masters

instagram.com/ellie_masters

bookbub.com/authors/ellie-masters

goodreads.com/Ellie_Masters

Connect with Ellie Masters

Website:
elliemasters.com
Purchase Direct:
elliemasters.com/shopify
Amazon Author Page:
elliemasters.com/amazon
Facebook:
elliemasters.com/Facebook
Goodreads:
elliemasters.com/Goodreads
Bookbub:
elliemasters.com/Bookbub
Instagram:
elliemasters.com/Instagram

Final Thoughts

I hope you enjoyed this book as much as I enjoyed writing it. If you enjoyed reading this story, please consider leaving a review on Amazon and Goodreads, and please let other people know. A sentence is all it takes. Friend recommendations are the strongest catalyst for readers' purchase decisions! And I'd love to be able to continue bringing the characters and stories from My-Mind-to-the-Page.

Second, call or e-mail a friend and tell them about this book. If you really want them to read it, gift it to them. If you prefer digital friends, please use the "Recommend" feature of Goodreads to spread the word.

Or visit my blog https://elliemasters.com, where you can find out more about my writing process and personal life.

Come visit The EDGE: Dark Discussions where we'll have a chance to talk about my works, their creation, and maybe what the future has in store for my writing.

Facebook Reader Group: Ellz Bellz

Thank you so much for your support!

Love,

Ellie

Dedication

This book is dedicated to you, my reader. Thank you for spending a few hours of your time with me. I wouldn't be able to write without you to cheer me on. Your wonderful words, your support, and your willingness to join me on this journey is a gift beyond measure.

Whether this is the first book of mine you've read, or if you've been with me since the very beginning, thank you for believing in me as I bring these characters 'from my mind to the page and into your hearts.'

Love,
Ellie

THE END

www.ingramcontent.com/pod-product-compliance
Lightning Source LLC
Chambersburg PA
CBHW031045310726
48969CB00007B/2128